HOUSE AT HAWK'S END

Also by Claudette Nicole

The Mistress of Orion Hall

Bloodroots Manor

Circle of Secrets

The Haunting of Drumroe

The Dark Mill

HOUSE AT HAWK'S END

CLAUDETTE NICOLE

ISBN-13: 978-1-957868-36-3

Published by
Cutting Edge Books
PO Box 8212
Calabasas, CA 91372
www.cuttingedgebooks.com

CHAPTER ONE

The land was marked with names that held the smell of the sea and the soul of the lonely.

But, the girl reminded herself, she had known it would be that way, had wanted it that way and had been pulled to it by an inner hunger. Wind's Head, Seal Island, Cape Glacier, Barren Land. The names flashed by again as the girl stood on the beach, her bare feet pressed into the white sand, the beige trench coat wrapped tightly around her slender shape. Hard and lonely names, all of them, and now, here, the loneliest of them all, the point called Hawk's End, a gnarled knuckle of land thrusting itself into the sea from the northernmost tip of Nova Scotia. But there's lonely and lonely, the girl told herself as she stood at the edge of the sand, a small figure facing the sea. Her hair, light brown and shoulder length, pulled out behind her in the wind as she watched the sea, gray green and excited by the coming storm, fling itself against the beach with thunderous delight.

Overhead, the seabirds swooped low, heading inshore as the storm neared, terns, gulls, a plover or two and sandpipers, always sandpipers. Their long, mournfully sharp cries cut through the sound of the surf. Why did seabirds never warble or chirp, the girl asked herself as she watched their long, swooping flight. Why was theirs always a lonely song? Did they forever cry in protest because they belonged neither to land nor to sea? Belonging, she sniffed. Now there was a word with a hundred meanings. Or was there only one? The spray whipped into her face and she tasted the salt with her tongue. She cast a glance at the sky, low with hurrying clouds, gray to the horizon, pressing down upon the sea. It was late afternoon and she had hurried to get here before dark, now doubly glad she had pushed herself as the wind whipped the tops of the waves. The storm, not more than a few hours away, would be a howler.

Pushing her shoes deeper into the pockets of her trench coat, she pressed her feet into the sand and turned left to where the beach stretched. She cast a glance back at the car sitting up on the edge of the dunes where she'd left it. She'd come back for it later. Now she would walk along the beach and taste its wild loneliness.

She turned up her coat collar and gazed ahead to where the beach ended and the rocks climbed up from the sea to the land, piled atop each other as they were casually flung by the giant hand of the sea. At the top of them, where the land leveled off, she could see the house, gray against gray, weathered wood against weathered sky, not more than a dark gray mass yet. She didn't hurry her steps. There would be plenty of time for the house at Hawk's End. Now was a time for savoring the wildness of the wind and the scudding clouds. The sea reached up to clutch at her ankles, icy water fed by the arctic stream, and she moved a few steps higher on the sand. To her left the thin beach rose up to the dunes, topped by a line of eelgrass and railroad vine. Suddenly the girl frowned and turned to look behind her. She was being watched. She felt it, eyes on her. But there was no one she could see and she slowly scanned the top of the dunes. Shrugging, she went on, unwilling to dwell on it. There had been too much to dwell on these past months. There was too much now.

The rocks loomed larger and soon she was upon them, being showered by the sea spray as the waves exploded on them. The house, set back from the edge of the land above, was no longer visible, but the girl saw the rocks made a set of disordered steps and she began to climb over the first ones. Pausing on a flat rock, she pressed her hands down on it and felt its strength, the smooth, cold, wet timelessness of it flowing through her fingers. Another wave broke and splattered her as she stood with her hands pressed to the rock, fingers of kelp rubbing against her skin. She saw a lobster pot slammed into the rocks, shattering at once. Her gaze scanned the rushing sea and the spare shoreline. Even without the storm's grayness this was indeed a bleak, harsh land, and suddenly she thought of all the soft-sanded, warm, lush beaches she had walked upon. Here, in this cold, desolate place, they seemed almost obscene. But this was the land she wanted, all the hard incorruptibility of it. She turned and began to climb up the rocks, finding the path as though she had done it every day. The wind pulled at her as she neared the top and she heard the crashing of the rising waves. Pausing, she peered back along the beach, now smaller, thinner, and hoped the car was on high enough ground. It was beyond sight, the beach and the dunes melting into a white-streaked gray. Pulling herself on, she climbed upward and then her fingers were closing over the edge of the soil as she reached the top. She heard her gasp torn from her by the wind.

The house at Hawk's End stood before her, no longer a dim, weather-shrouded shape but a torn and battered, stark and forbidding monstrosity. It rose up with two gables, things of hanging shutters and loose boards, a broken widow's walk around the edge of the second floor, gray brown streaked sides, a sagging roofline leading to the rear where a huge oak stood smashed into it, its lifeless branches rising up from the gaping hole. The front of the house appeared intact, save for hanging shutters and sides that waved and bulged and the girl felt herself shudder. It was not the smashed roof of the rear, not just the stark, cracked and broken sides. Had it been in perfect condition it would have still been monstrous, the girl felt; the house had a sharp, clutching look that not even its broken back could dissipate. She had expected a place in some disrepair but not this derelict house that sat waiting with a malevolence all its own.

Drawing a deep breath, she moved toward it, bending against the wind that pushed like an unseen hand against her. The windows at the front of the house had been cleaned, looking faintly incongruous, as polished buttons on a stained and tattered jacket. The front door was massive, black oak with a huge brass knocker in the shape of an anchor. The girl lifted the piece and let it fall against the door. Waiting, she gazed back to that part of the beach she could see. It was only a thin strip now as the sea's gathering fury claimed still more of it. Hearing a sound behind the door, she turned quickly as the door opened, expecting the sound of creaking hinges and a little disappointed when it swung open noiselessly. The figure that stood in the entrance towered over her in a black high-necked dress and a long gray apron. The woman's face was gaunt, made of angles, sharp and stiff as a pine board. Her jet black hair was pulled back tight on her head and worn in a bun, and her eyes were gray with flecks of green in them. The girl noticed her hands, coarse and reddened, hanging loosely from long, powerful arms.

"Hello. I'm Jean Burroughs," the girl said, trying to sound friendly and warm. The huge woman's eyes didn't flicker and the sharp, stiff face remained impassive. "You must be Mrs. Colburn," Jean tried again.

"I'm Amantha Colburn," the woman said, her voice as hard as her face. "You weren't to come for two days yet."

"I know, but I decided to come a little earlier," Jean said.

"You shouldn't have come at all," the big woman said. "But then—you had to come."

Jean felt her skin grow cold for an instant and she just managed to hold back the frown that tried to form on her brow. How did she know, Jean wondered as she stared at the big woman's impassive face. How did she know that was the way it was?

"Where are your bags?" Amantha Colburn asked.

"Back where the beach begins, where I left the car," Jean said.

"Better go back and get them. The storm will be here full by dark and that's not far off."

"All right," Jean said.

"There's a road runs along the top of the dunes, back from them a few yards," the woman said, and Jean caught her tongue again. *I know,* she'd almost said, but she didn't know, she'd never seen the road, and yet she *knew.*

"I'll leave the door unlatched. I was about to leave," Amantha Colburn said, and Jean, starting to turn, halted in surprise.

"I thought you were living here. I was told you were," she said.

"I won't stay here at night," the woman answered. "Not at night." She turned her broad back on the girl and walked back into the house. Jean looked after her a moment, not trying to hold back the frown now, and then hurried off, head low against the tearing wind. The road edging the dunes was near enough, and when she reached it, she turned to glance back at the house at Hawk's End. The newly cleaned windows seemed to be glaring eyes watching her, and again she was struck by the malevolence of the gray, tattered structure. It was as an unkempt old crone sitting on a rock and eying each passerby with a storehouse of venom.

The rain began as Jean Burroughs hurried down the road, hurled by the wind in cold, stinging needles. The light was fading fast as she neared the car, and she was almost at it when she saw the two figures on the road, crossing in front of her. They halted as she came up to them, and she saw the first was an old man wearing a fisherman's weather slicker, his eyes an angry blue in a parchment-skin face. He glared at her as he blocked her path. The girl looked past him to the second man and saw he was young, wearing a black turtleneck sweater. His face was strong with the strength of those who live by the sea, ruggedly handsome, with eyes almost as black as the onyx hair that curled naturally over his forehead. His deep eyes held hers and she thought she saw a question in them. Or was she imagining things? The old man's voice brought her attention back to him.

"So you're here," he said, biting out the words. "We heard you were coming."

Jean felt her temper flare. "I didn't think my coming would be such a major event," she snapped and was instantly sorry she had sounded so shrewish.

"It won't make any difference," the old man said. "We know why you've come, and it won't change things."

"You don't know anything of the sort and you're making absolutely no sense to me," Jean answered. "Just who are you, anyway?"

The old man opened his mouth to answer when the other, younger one moved forward, his voice deep, rich, but walking on the edge of command.

"Enough, Enoch," he said. The old man's lips closed in a tight line but the anger stayed in his eyes as he turned and walked away. Jean Burroughs met the younger man's probing black brown eyes with her own frown. She saw his eyes move across her face, taking in the short, straight line of her nose, the soft curve of her cheeks and the fullness of her lips. Then, abruptly, he turned to look out at the white-flecked gray that was the sea. "There's no time to talk now with the storm showing its face," he said, speaking into the wind. Giving her another glance, he turned and left her, and she saw the old man waiting. They walked on together, disappearing into the rain by the time she reached the car. She wondered if theirs had been the eyes she had felt on her when she stood on the beach. Inside the car, out of the driving rain and wind, her anger subsided quickly and she wondered if she hadn't been too curt. After all, any newcomer in a small place such as Hawk's End would cause a stir. She'd driven through the little village, hardly more than a half-dozen blocks long, just before reaching the beach. But then, Jean reflected as she drove slowly along the dune road, there had been more than casual attention in the old man's angry eyes. Her welcome to Hawk's End had so far been a strange one indeed. Amantha Colburn's uncannily accurate remark, the obvious hate in an old fisherman's eyes and a fast-descending northeaster. And the house at Hawk's End, a shattered, battered derelict that quivered with its own strange presence.

The rain, harder now, made puddles on the road and she had to concentrate on driving the little Ford, circa 1955. She'd never felt the need for her own car until now. When she was sure she was coming to Hawk's End, she'd picked this one up in a used-car lot for virtually nothing. With a touch of grimness in her smile she reflected that it seemed to fit in perfectly here at Hawk's End. Drawing up to the great, gray overhang of the house, she parked in front of the door and hurried her bags inside in short, fast relays. The light was fast disappearing and the wind and rain were angry, tearing things now. Inside the house, in the dark foyer, she halted and listened to the sound of the place as it creaked and groaned. Dimly she made out a huge room, a library once, to the right of the wide entranceway. Its shelves, now only half-filled with books, presented a series of toothless grimaces. Turning, she saw a living room with a fireplace at one end and freshly cut wood stacked by it. Hurrying in, she found paper beside the wood and got a fire started in the fireplace, holding her arms across her chest in an effort to keep warm until the flames began to grow. Finally they took hold and the room lighted with the dancing illumination they cast about. There were old, deep chairs and a big sofa of faded green. She glimpsed ancient drapes on the windows and a coffee table at one side. But the room had been cleaned and put into some semblance of presentableness. Jean pulled and pushed on the big sofa until it was centered in front of the fireplace. Perspiring now in the warmth of the fire, she took off her coat and went into the blackness of the rest of the house to latch the front door, thinking how quite ridiculous that was in view of the gaping hole in the roof at the rear of the house.

The short walk to the front door was a journey into a cold, damp world, and she hurried back to the warmth of the fire, glancing once again back at the blackness of the foyer and the dimly outlined stairway leading to the second floor. There seemed no provision for lights anywhere, and Jean made a mental note to inquire about that first thing in the morning. *Damn,* she said silently. *Why couldn't that woman have waited till I got back?*

Curling up on the sofa, she put another thick log on the fire and felt the heat rise at once. Taking off her skirt and sweater, she opened her smaller suitcase and took out a loose-fitting, short flannel nightie, red with white trim. She slipped it on over her bra and panties, settled down on the sofa, and let the yellow and red and blue-tipped flames dance her into relaxing. If she didn't get up to glance over the edge of the sofa at the yawning blackness behind her, she could almost feel cozy and so she pushed herself deeper into the soft cushions and concentrated on the fire. The northeaster was in full howl now, driving sheets of cold rain against the old house, making it groan and creak in protest. Staring into the fire, Jean let it shut out the storm, too, and in the dancing flames she saw old faces, old friends, all that which had suddenly become too much of everything and too much of nothing, a world full of emptiness. They were there, crystal clear in the flames, all those who had made up that world. She heard the sound of it, too, and saw herself in the flames, running like the others, from place to place, arms to arms, bed to bed. The sounds drifted out to her from the firelight, soft, then strong, receding and coming on again, as though someone were twisting the volume dial on a radio.

"Did you hear, Dulcie's moved in with Bill?"

"Are you going to Paul's affair? Don't bring a lot to wear. You won't be needing much."

"Stay with me, Tom. You don't really care if Charlotte knows."

"Where's Howard? On the terrace with that bitch Harriet, I'll bet."

"Let's not ruin a lovely relationship by getting serious."

The voices drifted away but they were there in that world she had left, and she would be with them still if it hadn't all exploded for her in a scalding moment of bitter reality. Suddenly, in pain and inner agony, that world had exploded around her and it had never been the same again. Not that she hadn't tried. It just hadn't worked, not for her, anyway. The others were stronger, perhaps, or were they weaker? In any case they kept that world going, with renewed desperation, she suspected. But for her it was impossible. All the king's parties and all the king's drinks, couldn't put it back together again. Then, on a moonless night in her very small but very posh apartment on Boston's Beacon Hill, it had come to her, a sudden flashing thing that made her wake in the dead of the night. She remembered how she had sat up in bed, naked, automatically glancing down to see if she were alone there and then sitting with her body quivering, knowing what she had to do, as though she had been called. The next morning she had gone to the firm of Bancroft and Company that handled the few bits and pieces of her father's estate, what had been left to leave to her, a few stocks and bonds, a deed or two, and the house at Hawk's End.

"Why, of course the house is still yours, Miss Burroughs," Mr. Bancroft had said. "There's land, too, along the water, but I can't see why a lovely young woman such as yourself would want to go there. It's my understanding it's worthless for anything except sea gulls and fishermen. Weatherby and Weatherby have informed me the house is in considerable disrepair."

"Who are they?" Jean had asked.

"A small law firm in the town of Hawk's End," the broker had said. "They've handled whatever local taxes have come up and sort of kept an eye on the property. We've paid them out of dividends from the few shares of stock we hold from the estate. I'm afraid that's about run out, though."

"Phone this Weatherby and Weatherby," Jean had said then. "Tell them I'm going to live there at Hawk's End, for a while, anyway. Have them hire a housekeeper to open up the place. I'll give you a check for that."

She saw Mr. Bancroft's frown again. "Your father bought the place at a tax sale fifty years ago," the man had said. "He and your mother went there one summer and left in a week and that was forty years ago. Altogether, the house hasn't been lived in for some hundred and fifty years. Your father held onto the place because he hoped someday he might get a buyer, but of course he never did. I still can't fathom why, Miss Burroughs, you want to live in a derelict old house in a grim, isolated spot."

"I have my reasons," she said, not hiding the curtness of her answer. And she did have reasons, all right, enough for a hundred souls to carry. Running away, some of her friends might have given as a reason, and maybe they were right, maybe it was just another kind of running. But why here, to Hawk's End? Why had the name wakened her that moonless night in her apartment to reverberate in her mind like the sound of a gong? Her only answer was that the mind works in its own strange ways, opening up doors of its own at the most unexpected times. And so, whether running or finding, seeking or knowing, she had come here and left all the rest behind, crammed away in a corner of her mind. But, of course, the yesterdays never stayed crammed away. They kept popping out all the time. But perhaps, here, in time, they would fade away. Suddenly she felt terribly tired, felt her eyes closing in the warmth of the firelight. She had pushed herself hard to get here by the afternoon's end and now the girl's long, slim body stretched itself out on the big sofa, the nightgown slipping up to let the firelight dance on her shapely legs, softly contoured and firm. Sleep, the sleep of the exhausted, stole over her, and she lay still, glowing in beauty by the light of the flames.

The fire had died down to flickering embers and cold had seized the room when Jean woke, sitting up suddenly as she had that moonless night in Boston. A cold perspiration was on her, and she heard the sound of loose shutters slamming against the sides of the house. Outside, the storm still raged and the old house seemed to sway and cry out, and she suddenly knew she was not alone. Swinging her long legs from the sofa, she got to her feet and peered into the blackness of the doorway and the foyer. The wind whistled and then there was another sound, a cry, a moaning that at first she took as the wind. But then the wind made its own howling sound and the other rose above it, a sound not frightening, yet filled with fear, not threatening, yet filled with menace. Then she heard the footsteps, dragging steps, running, then halting, then running again. Jean's eyes went to the ceiling as the sounds seemed to move above her, toward the edge of the room, then on the creaking steps, and she felt her body quivering.

"Who's there?" Jean called out and heard the footsteps cease only to begin their strange dragging sound a moment later. The soft calling rose again, high, then low, undulating like the voices of some strange Greek chorus.

"Who's there? Who's out there?" Jean called again. The house seemed to bend with a blast of wind, and Jean delved into her opened suitcase, bringing out the powerful flashlight she had brought with her. Long-handled and heavy, it would be a good weapon, too, she told herself as she switched it on and moved toward the black foyer. The light streamed forward, picking out the entranceway, the side of the dark wood door molding and then the hall as she reached the door. The sounds seemed to be coming from above, on the second-floor landing, and she turned the flashlight upward, letting the beam pick its way up the steps. The light made each piece of worn carpeting seem more worn, more torn, each a tiny testimonial to decay. She swung the light to follow the smooth wood of the straight banister, up to the second floor landing where it revealed only the walls of the landing. The soft calling had stopped, as had the sounds of something moving, and only the wind howled outside now. She turned the light from the stairway to the wide hallway that ran back along the side of the stairs, following the white finger as it showed only the empty hall. Jean moved a few steps down the hall alongside the stairs, scanning with the flashlight. Then, suddenly, the sound came again, a scraping, dragging, then faster movements. It was coming from directly overhead, on the second-floor landing, unmistakable this time and she whirled, swinging the beam upward.

Just as she did so, she heard the sound of old wood splintering, tearing away, and the light revealed the heavy cornerpost of the second-story balustrade as it began to topple with deceptive slowness first, then terrifying speed. The girl saw the rounded cornerpost coming down on her and her feet seemed rooted to the spot. Then, with a cry of terror, she flung herself backward against the wall just as the heavy piece smashed to the floor with shattering force. Small slivers of wood hit her face as she stood pressed against the wall, inches away from the falling death that would have smashed in her skull. There was only silence now, save for the rasping sound of her own breathing, breaths so deeply drawn she felt her young, full breasts pull against the nightgown with each one. There was silence for a long moment when even the storm outside seemed to pause for breath, and, her hand shaking, she turned the flashlight up to shine on the second-floor landing. The light revealed the broken bottom of the cornerpost where it had torn loose. That and nothing more. Jean lowered the light and moved back into the living room, half-running to the sofa to cling there until her body ceased to shake. The storm had taken on its fury again, slamming loose boards and shutters against the sides of the old house like so many firecrackers going off. Jean found she was shivering from the cold, and she put more logs on the fire and stood before it as it blazed into life again. Then, the warmth coating her body, she lay back on the sofa again.

Death had missed her by a fraction, and she sat still and listened to the sounds of the old house. Only the groan of it against the wind now. The long, undulating, crying sounds were gone and the footsteps with them. Had it all been some animal in from the storm, moving about in fear? The light could well have missed an animal cowering in a corner of the landing and then it might have run, smashing against the rotted wood of the cornerpost. That would have been enough to topple it, she explained to herself. Yes, it had to have been something like that, she told herself with firm logic. The cold perspiration that was on her as she wakened, the strange presence she had felt in the house, that was all her own exhaustion working overtime. No matter, Jean said to herself. She was here, and regardless of what Amantha Colburn had meant, the woman had been right, she'd had to come. And she had her reasons, the very clear ones and those less clear but equally valid, equally effective.

Jean settled back on the cushions of the sofa again and listened to the storm begin slowly to lose its fury. She was asleep when the wind died away and the old house ceased to creak. The rotted cornerpost lay where it had fallen, and slowly the stormy night slipped away.

CHAPTER TWO

The morning came in still gray but without the wind and the rain. Jean woke as the light of the day moved over her sleeping form, and she dressed quickly, shivering in the dampness. Throwing on slacks and a sweater, she got up and went into the foyer, pausing to look at the heavy cornerpost where it lay, shuddering when she did so. She skirted it and went down the hallway, finding the kitchen just where she was certain it would be, on the left. It was old-fashioned in every detail, from the wide floorboards to the iron stove and the thick wooden work areas on each side of a big sink. A big butcher's block stood in the center of the spacious room, and opening the wooden cupboards, Jean saw that some supplies had been laid in. She found tea and some thick mugs and an iron kettle, a tin of biscuits and some butter, the last in an old icebox. She breakfasted and returned to the living room to peer out the windows at the vista of the sea that stretched out before her. Part of the beach was visible, too, and she saw that the angry waters had lessened and were rolling onto the shore with only occasional violence. The sea had given back the beach again, she noted, the white sand taking on brightness as the sun tried to move through the breaking grayness. A heavy sound that took her a moment to identify turned out to be the door knocker and she hurried to admit Amantha Colburn. The huge woman's gaunt face was as impassive as the day before, and her eyes scanned the girl quickly, as though she were searching for some sign. Stepping into the hallway, she halted as she saw the fallen cornerpost where it lay.

"It came loose and fell during the night," Jean explained. "It nearly killed me."

Amantha Colburn's gaze fixed itself on the girl for a long moment, and then the woman removed her coat, hanging it on a hook in the hallway.

"Is there a carpenter in town who can come and put up a new cornerpost?" Jean asked. "Anything will do. The top of the banister is just hanging loose now. I don't want that tearing off, too."

"I'll call Fred Lester," the woman said.

"Don't tell me we've a telephone here," Jean said, unable to hide the angry sarcasm of her feelings. "How about electricity?"

"There's a phone line," Amantha Colburn said as Jean followed her into the kitchen. "Mr. Weatherby had one connected when he heard you were coming. Phone's in the library. No electricity. Never been any lines put through here to the house."

The woman opened a big closet just outside the kitchen, and Jean saw the rows of hurricane lamps on the two top shelves.

"I'll have these filled and put them around the house," Amantha Colburn said. "They give a good strong light. No need for any upstairs. Your room's down here, down the hall."

"When the man comes to fix a new cornerpost have him check out the stairway and the rest of the railing there," Jean said. "I don't want any more accidents. I heard noises last night, some animal up there getting out of the storm. He must have hit the post and that was enough to send it falling."

Amantha Colburn was looking at her with that long, unfathomable stare again, Jean saw, a stare that seemed to go right through her.

"No animal," the woman said, turning away and preparing to get to work, taking dust cloths from under the sink.

"Of course it was an animal. I heard it," Jean said. Amantha Colburn paused on her way from the kitchen to fix the girl with another long stare.

"No animal," the woman said and turned away, moving from the room. Jean felt her lips tighten. The woman had an irritating manner as she made remarks with an unbending certainty, as though she held some secret wisdom. Annoyed, Jean went into the hall and saw the woman standing by the fallen cornerpost, staring down at it.

"Which is the room you've readied for me?" Jean asked, annoyance in her voice. "Is there a bath with it?"

Amantha Colburn nodded slowly and led the way to a room at the end of the hall, just before another, back stairway that went up to the smashed-in roof at the rear of the house. The room was large enough with an old four-poster bed in it, fresh linens on the bed and a small bathroom on the right. A beautifully carved old chest stood against one wall and a fine oaken table took up the center of the floor. A fireplace lined the east wall of the room.

"Are the fireplaces the only heat?" Jean asked. "Is there any other hot water source?"

"There's a wood-burning, hot water heater in the cellar," the woman said. "It's on. You'll find the water hot enough."

Jean nodded and followed the big woman out of the room, deciding to take a bath after she went down to the beach for a walk in the early day. At the foot of the stairs she saw the woman glance up for a moment and then go into the library. A moment of annoyance flaring in her again, Jean turned and started up the stairs, touching the banister lightly with her hand and feeling it shake. As she neared the top of the stairs she saw the layer of dust that covered the steps and the floor, a thin carpet of undisturbed gray. Her footsteps on it left clear marks and sent small whirls of dust softly scurrying along the floor. She halted when she reached the second-floor landing and gazed at the broken wood base of the cornerpost. A chill enveloped her body, and Jean felt herself standing very still, finding difficulty in swallowing. The thin layer of gray dust was undisturbed, without a mark on it, and Jean glanced back at her own footsteps so clearly outlined in the dust. An animal up here, any animal and certainly one heavy enough to smash the cornerpost loose, would have had to leave its tracks in the dust. The realization danced in her mind with a mocking insistence that would have been mischievous were it not so frightening.

Turning quickly, Jean hurried down the stairs with her mind whirling. There *had* been something on the landing in the night, something in the house. She'd heard it and felt its presence. Perhaps the wind had blown a new layer of dust over the floor, covering its tracks, Jean told herself, and knew instantly that she'd never be satisfied with that glib explanation. At the library door she saw Amantha Colburn standing there, watching her, the woman's stare impassive.

"Why did you say it was no animal, Amantha?" Jean asked, frowning.

"I just knew," the woman said flatly.

"You think the cornerpost just came loose and fell, then," Jean questioned and saw the woman's quick shrug that said nothing.

Jean swallowed her annoyance at the woman's taciturn resistance to being friendly, and she hurried out of the house. Outside, the cool morning wind helped to blow away her annoyance. It was probably nothing more than the big woman's way, a secretive personality, the kind that enjoyed feeling secretly wise. Jean walked along the dune road and saw the sun coming through the clouds, lighting the beach with a warm brightness. Jean saw a dory pulled up onto the sand and a figure near it, pulling in loose lobster pot lines broken by the storm. She found a gentle slope and went down it to the beach. Only when she neared the figure did she see it was the young, black-haired man she'd met on the road yesterday. He turned as she approached, his black eyes meeting hers, questions in them again, and then he turned back to his work. He had a pile of lines and broken lobster pots gathered on the sand, Jean saw as she reached him.

The dory was bigger and heavier than it had seemed from a distance, carrying thick oars and a small outboard motor at the rear.

"Good morning," she called out cheerily. He looked at her as she halted, leaning against the gunwale of the dory. His rugged, strong face stayed unsmiling, but he allowed a small answering nod. Jean watched him as he untangled lines, pulled in others, bending and working with an easy rhythm and grace, strong hands and powerful arms, the sleeves of the black turtleneck sweater pushed up, unmindful of the chilling sea breeze. The sun caught the yellow and red-tipped lobster pot buoys and gave them an added note of brightness. Spread on the sand, they were like huge jewels on a cloth.

"Where's your friend?" Jean asked, leaning against the dory as the man moved a few paces away to fold the lines with effortless artistry.

"Enoch? He'll be along," he said, glancing at her. "If not, I'll pick him up around the point."

He was handsome, Jean decided, handsome with vibrant strength, the uncompromising honesty that was in the seaswept rocks of the shore. As she continued to watch him work he suddenly paused, his black eyes softening but his strong face still unsmiling.

"What are you thinking?" he asked, the question taking her by surprise. She smiled back at his seriousness.

"Just that those lines and lobster buoys are an extension of you," she replied. "I was thinking of a saying the French have about those who have been injured at their work. The craft has entered their flesh, they say. It's true about those who are such a part of their work, too."

He watched her, a moment of reflection deepening his eyes. "I expect it might be," he said in his deep, rich voice. Short sentences and a frugality with words seemed to be part of the people here, Jean decided. But there was something welcome in that. It gave deeper meaning to their words, making them seem to count more, and she thought of the endless, meaningless chatter of that other world she'd left.

"Who are you?" Jean asked the man. "You seem to know just who I am, so I think I ought to know you."

He stopped in his work to hold her eyes with a steady stare. "I'm Ferris Duncan," he said. "Like most everyone here, I'm a fisherman."

"What was your friend Enoch so angry about yesterday?" Jean asked. "Why did my being here seem to annoy him?"

"Did old man Weatherby send for you?" Ferris Duncan answered, returning to his work as he asked the question. Jean felt her temper rising again.

"Nobody sent for me," she snapped. "I came on my own, because I wanted to come here, because that old wreck of a house happens to be mine."

Jean saw Ferris Duncan halt in his folding of the lines, straighten up, and turn to face her, his eyes direct, almost burning in their intensity. "What are you punishing yourself for?" he asked slowly.

Jean felt the rush of color to her face and hated herself for it, hoping quickly he would take it as anger.

"I—I'm not punishing myself for anything," she said, hating herself for falling over her words. "What makes you think a thing like that?"

"There's nothing for you here," he said, his flat certainty an echo of Amantha Colburn's all-knowing tone, and Jean's brown eyes narrowed in anger.

"Isn't that rather presumptuous of you?" she threw back at the big man's rocklike figure. "It so happens that there are things I very much want here."

"Not want," he said. "Need."

He could use words like harpoons, this big, rough-hewn man, and Jean found herself glaring at him. They exchanged silences, his deep eyes searching her face, as she desperately tried to find the right words to answer him.

"There's strength here," she finally said. Strength to draw upon, she almost added.

"There's hardness here," he answered. "The sea lets for no mistakes and the land gives up nothing. It's an unforgiving place, this. Everything comes hard here, even tears. It doesn't let a man hide from anything or anyone, most of all himself."

"You think that's what I want here, to hide from something?"

He didn't answer, but his eyes held hers in a steady gaze. "You're so much a part of things here you can't see that there's beauty in its hardness," Jean said.

She saw a smile, a quick, rueful smile, touch his face and was surprised by the moment of captivating charm it brought. "I can see beauty," Ferris Duncan said. "And I know its beauty well. It's a hard beauty, the kind that stays after everything else is washed away."

"But it's there. It's real."

The smile came again, just as brief. "Yes, it's real," he said. "And I see your beauty and that's real enough, too. It's enough to light the night but it's not for this land."

"Meaning exactly what?" Jean asked.

"A thistle will bloom where a mayflower will die," he said. "There's not hardness enough in your beauty. You're soft earth and quiet, shaded places, the side of a brook maybe, in a wooded glen."

"You could be wrong," Jean said, hearing the defiance in her voice, and the hope in that defiance.

"I could be," he said unsmiling, meaning he was certain he wasn't. He turned, and gathering up the lines and lobster pot buoys, he put them in the dory. He was inside the boat with one quick leap, securing them, and then back onto the sand again. Suddenly she didn't want him to go. This rugged man who made every word count held everything she'd come up here to gather to herself.

"Must you go?" she asked, and he paused, his hands against the prow of the dory.

"Enoch will be waiting around the point. The point down from here, not the one of your cove," he said, and there was a sudden hardness in his eyes and his voice.

"What do you mean by that?" Jean asked. Ferris Duncan's eyes darkened.

"You're a strange one," he said. "I wonder if maybe you don't really know."

"Know what? Why Mr. Weatherby is supposed to have sent for me? No, I don't know," Jean said.

"Then you'd best find out," Ferris Duncan said, putting his shoulder to the dory and giving it a hard push. The boat slid from the sand into the surf, and he was in it with a powerful bound, the oars in his hands at once, rowing out through the surf. She watched him go, bobbing on the incoming breakers, riding over them and then, out a little further turning on the outboard motor. She waved a hand at him as the dory made a circle and headed out to sea. He kept his hand on the tiller but she could feel his eyes on her. When the boat was but a small dot on the rolling sea, she turned and headed back to the house. A talk with Mr. Weatherby was definitely on her agenda for the afternoon, she decided. Everyone seemed to have their own ideas why she was here at Hawk's End, she told herself grimly, when they were all so far from knowing the real reasons that had sent her here. But even as the thought held her mind for a moment, she saw herself again sitting up in bed that night in her apartment, knowing at once she had to come here to Hawk's End. Were there reasons beyond those she had herself, she wondered? Weren't hers more than enough? Shaking away the thought, she reached the dune road again and headed back to the house. As she approached the gray, waiting structure, its cackling malevolence seemed to reach out to her, and she felt her skin crawl in a moment of sudden chill.

The sound of hammering echoed through the thick door as she neared, and pushing it open, she saw the man on the second-floor landing, putting a temporary cornerpiece of plain white pine in place, hardly more than a bridge to hold the banister and the landing rail together. He glanced down at her and continued with his work. Amantha Colburn was in the kitchen as she passed, and Jean stopped in the doorway.

"Amantha, is there a cove of some sort that's part of this property?" Jean asked. She saw the big woman turn to her, the gaunt face hard, her eyes narrowed.

"You don't know that?" the woman returned, and Jean let her temper go.

"Dammit, I wouldn't ask then!" she snapped and saw the woman's eyes narrow, their gray taking on the color of ice under a winter sky.

"The cove is past the house, at the very end of the land," the woman said. "Just walk beyond the house, north. You'll come to it."

"Thank you," Jean said, a thin frost in her voice. "I'm going to take a hot bath, first, change, and have a look. This afternoon I want to go to town and see Mr. Weatherby."

"I'll stay through dinner if you'll be back in time," Amantha said. "I've a small roast."

"I'll be back," Jean said and saw the big woman's eyes lower as she turned away, almost as if they were afraid to show friendliness.

"There's mail for you," Amantha Colburn said, not looking up. "On the table in the library, the small one by the door."

"Mail!" Jean echoed, frowning, and then she was hurrying off into the library, scooping the letter from the table. It would be Ted, of course. He'd been the only one from that other world she'd told where she was going. She walked back to her room, holding the letter in her hand, seeing Ted's wide, genial face before her, his sandy, unruly hair and hazel eyes. Ted had helped a lot during the past month. They'd never been anything but friends, but they'd grown to be very close friends. Ted Holbrook was the soul of charm and wit. He could use irony, sarcasm, and charm and make them into his own unique blend. He was also one of the top photographers in the magazine and fashion world. He'd be the very top one if he buckled down to really working at it, as she had often told him. But anything more than a minimum of work was "depressing, distracting, dull," as he put it. Ted was completely devoted to the pleasure principle, but unlike the others, who seemed to work at it with such desperation, Ted lived the philosophy with the easy charm of the true believer. He had been the most understanding and, surprisingly, the most tender and, certainly, the most concerned, and she was grateful to him. When she'd told him she was going away to be alone, he'd charmed the address from her, promising to write every day. She'd taken that as just another of his blithe good intentions but had appreciated the thought anyway.

She put the envelope down on the edge of the bathroom sink and ran her bath; the water was hotter than she had dared hope. In the faded mirror on the wall she glimpsed the long, lovely slenderness of her body, its smooth, small-waisted delicate curving. Being attractive, being desired, had always been a gift she had taken for granted. Then, suddenly, she had come to learn that it was a gift that contained the seeds of a terrible responsibility. She sank down into the deep, spacious old tub and let the warm water caress her. Reaching up, she took the letter from the edge of the sink and opened it, remembering how Ted had tried to dissuade her from going off alone. He was, she quickly saw, one of those people who could make himself come alive in his letters. She read eagerly, a slight smile touching her lips.

Dear Jeanie girl:

How goes all at the monastery? Or is it convent? Long silences and thrice-daily periods of meditation? I expect nothing less, my girl, nothing less. After all, you left us all to do it your way. When you return I expect you to be full of deep thoughts and meaningful philosophies, a girl of new depths. Frankly, I never saw much wrong with the old one.

Boston is humming with new energy as it always is at this time of the year. The robins fly south and the Harvard students come north. The usual people are giving all the usual parties. I was even trapped into accepting a new assignment at one of them which is a new low in sneakiness.

The leaves are blowing down the streets and the Common is taking on that wintry look. But I know where the dry martini dwells and the whiskey sour waits. You take care of yourself, hear me, girl? Say hello to the other monks for me.

Love,
Ted

Jean put the letter aside and finished her bath, feeling warm inside as well as outside. Dressing in a skirt of deep red and a gray, nubby sweater flecked with brown, she went outside to the hallway and saw that the temporary cornerpost was in place and the workman had left. Amantha Colburn was at the kitchen doorway, and Jean saw the woman's eyes take in her loveliness. For a moment it seemed as though Amantha Colburn might even say something nice and friendly, but the moment slipped past. "Dinner no later then six thirty," the woman said flatly.

"I'll remember," Jean said, and then, pausing in front of the woman, she threw out the question abruptly. "Why won't you stay here after dark, Amantha?" she asked.

The big woman's eyes met hers, expressionless, veiled.

"The others old Weatherby asked in town wouldn't come at all," Amantha said. "I don't live in town. I don't mix with them. I make my own way."

She turned and went down the hallway, picking up a mop she'd had behind the kitchen door, and Jean knew she had gotten all the answer she was going to get, for the time being, anyway. The girl went out into the morning and looked out across the sea. There were still clouds that raced along, but the sun darted out between them to make the blue of the water sparkle in spots, as though huge sequins had been carelessly tossed onto a blue cloth. She went to the edge of the level land where the rocks made their ragged steps down to the water, and then she turned north to walk along a narrow pathway that went past the house. Glancing up, she saw the huge oak that lay smashed into the rear of the house. The torn wood of the house seemed to have wrapped itself around the tree as though embracing it. Beyond the house the path curved slightly toward the sea and then suddenly the cove lay in front of her, much larger, much wider, and no doubt much deeper than she had expected it would be. She'd expected a small half-moon of land but this was a deep-water cove, full and spacious.

"Not your cove," Ferris Duncan had said and she heard the bitterness in his voice again. Why not her cove, she wondered. Why had he made it plain he was not meeting Enoch at her cove? Still turning the question over in her mind as she gazed down at the cove, she heard a sound behind her and turned quickly. A young man was coming toward her and he waved a hand at her. Wearing a brown hounds tooth jacket and dark brown trousers, he had sharp, alert eyes and an even-featured, friendly face, not with Ferris Duncan's rugged strength but definitely attractive.

"Hello," he called out as he neared her. "I'm Bob Weatherby." Jean saw him halt, and his eyes, brown and bright, probe hers. "You're frowning," he said. "I seem to have surprised you."

"I'm sorry," she laughed. "I just expected an older man."

"That'd be my father. He really runs the firm of Weatherby and Weatherby," the young man answered, his smile warm. "But you're not the only one surprised. I didn't expect to see anyone quite so lovely. Mrs. Colburn told me you'd gone walking back this way."

She liked the way he didn't give her a chance to reply to his compliment, going quickly past what was often an awkward moment. "You weren't expected till tomorrow so we weren't on hand to meet you. I'm sorry about that. Especially now that I've met you."

His grin was quick, infectious. "That's all right," Jean said. "I'm here, in one piece, and I've been welcomed, if you can call it that." Bob Weatherby grimaced.

"Amantha, you mean," he said. "She's the best we could do, I'm afraid."

"Not just Amantha," Jean said. "I've the feeling my coming here isn't at all welcome. In fact, there seems to be some kind of general belief that your father sent for me. I haven't the faintest notion why anyone thinks that but they seem to."

Bob Weatherby's smile was rueful again. "I'd rather let my father go into that with you," he said. "Why don't you drive into town with me and meet him?"

"Wonderful," Jean agreed. "I was going to do that myself this afternoon. My curiosity's been aroused, frankly, and people here have a way of talking around things."

"I know just what you mean," he laughed as they walked back to the house. He was instantly likable, she decided, a combination of pleasant affability and probing intelligence. His car, parked alongside hers, was almost as old, she noted as he opened the door for her. She saw his glance linger a moment on the smooth, long line of her legs and she smiled to herself. He drove up across the very tip of the land and pointed out the direction of Cabot Strait, which separated them from Newfoundland.

Skirting the edge of the cove, he cut back along narrow roads meant for buggies. Jean let her eyes roam across the windswept land, rising in the center, mostly rocks and sparse grass, yet with a bleak beauty to it all, a victorious kind of beauty that defied the world for being there at all.

"I'm sorry town isn't farther away," Bob Weatherby said as they rolled into the neat, ordered streets of the little village that bordered the water. Jean smiled in thanks and watched the square, wood houses go by, the people on the streets all touched by the wind and the sea, the men leathered, straight, the women carrying a quiet patience with them. As the car halted before a small white building, Jean saw the neat little sign on the window of the ground-floor office: WEATHERBY & WEATHERBY. A few people glanced at her as she got out of the car, their eyes hard, impassive, and she decided that this was characteristic of these people. Bob Weatherby, at her side, touched her elbow.

"Before we go in," he said, "I wonder if, seeing as how you'll stay for a while, you'd have dinner with me tomorrow night. Frankly it's been a long time since I've seen anything as pretty as you."

Jean laughed. "You have the same directness as everyone else here, yet you're different in a way, more sophisticated, shall we say."

"That's because I've only been back six months," he said. "My father asked me to come back and help him with some things. I've been practicing in Halifax for the past two years." Jean noticed a small tight line edge his mouth for a moment.

"I take it you didn't care for Halifax," she said.

"It seems they had enough young lawyers there," he said and let his smile take the edge from his words. "But you haven't answered my question."

"About dinner tomorrow night?" she echoed, thinking quickly. She hadn't come here to Hawk's End for dating, but then perhaps it was wrong to shut out everything. "All right, I'd be happy to," she said and watched his face brighten. Bob Weatherby had his own kind of good looks and a puppydog kind of eagerness that was most winning. He opened the door of the office for her and half-whispered in her ear as they entered.

"Father's of the old school," he said. "He's been called hard, but it's just that he doesn't believe in compromise."

Jean saw a neat office of dark, wood paneling and old-fashioned, heavy furniture that spoke of another age. Behind a wood railing, a middle-aged woman sat in front of a typewriter and glanced up as Bob ushered Jean past her and into an inner office. "The lion's den," he whispered as he opened the door. Jean saw the man rise from behind the desk of the larger, more richly furnished room. White-haired with a firm-skinned, ruddy face, his small, blue eyes were quick and shrewd. His mouth turned upward in a welcoming smile but not before she had caught the firm, set line of it. Jean took the extended hand as the man, fairly tall, came around the desk.

"Welcome to Hawk's End, Miss Burroughs," he said. "I'm Hobart Weatherby."

"Jean, Miss Burroughs, that is," Bob said quickly, "has a few questions for us."

"Be glad to answer them. I've a few questions for you, too, young woman," Hobart Weatherby said, drawing up a wide-bottomed, comfortable wooden chair for the girl. "You know, I'd thought that the house at Hawk's End was in for being abandoned altogether," the lawyer said, sitting down behind his desk and fixing Jean with a genial smile. "And now, suddenly, I find that there's an owner who wants to be a tenant."

"Just for a little while," Jean said. "I don't know that I could live there for long, at least not in its present condition. There's something depressing, almost threatening, about the place."

Hobart Weatherby chuckled. "It is an unattractive old place," he said. "But even so, in another place, with the land that's part of it, it would be valuable. Up here, it's been of no value at all, and

I'm afraid it never will be, unless you want to move in and make it livable."

Jean grimaced at the thought. It would take more than fresh paint and repairs, she knew. She didn't know what else, but she knew it would take something more.

"Jean's been told, rumor has it, that you asked her to come up here to Hawk's End. Folks have been unfriendly, to put it mildly."

Hobart Weatherby smiled, a genial smile that somehow was something less than genial. "People here aren't too friendly to start with, Miss Burroughs," he said to Jean. "In your case there's an even greater antagonism. It's been there for some while, but you, of course, knew nothing of it. I'm afraid I've been bearing the force of it, and frankly it doesn't bother me at all. It's all tied up with fishing rights."

Hobart Weatherby smiled again at Jean's frown of confusion. "Most everyone here earns their living fishing," he went on. "Fishing is the area's dominant industry. In fact, it's just about the only one. For the past few years the fishing along the coastline here has been very poor. But these stubborn, short-sighted people can't seem to understand that it's their own fault. They've depleted the fishing grounds by overfishing, by careless practices, by netting too many of the young fish, by not giving an area time to rest and become a feeding ground again."

"The fish have, however, taken to the deep water in the cove that's part of your property," Bob Weatherby cut in. "As the deed for the land specifies that the cove itself is part of the property, Father's never consented to letting them fish there. It didn't matter much when the coastal fishing was good, but now it's become a very sore point."

"I just felt that as overseer of the property I'd no right to let them fish it," Hobart Weatherby said. "I've a few other smaller inlets down the shore I administer, and I've never let them use those either. Besides, they'd do the same thing there they did along the coastal fishing grounds. They'd use the same stupid methods and deplete the areas until they'd have no industry left at all. Of course, they won't realize this, my dear. They're rather simple people who can neither see nor understand much beyond their own shortsighted views." Jean thought of Ferris Duncan as Hobart Weatherby spoke. She could see him as being stubborn and hard. But shortsighted and simple? No, that didn't seem to fit, not Ferris, at least. In fact, he had seemed quite perceptive. But then, perhaps he was not representative of the others. Bob's voice brought her attention back.

"It's not a question of their not being able to fish," he said. "They just have to go out to sea a bit farther. But naturally, they want the easiest fishing closest to shore. Actually, Father's trying to do what's best for them. Letting them fish the cove and continue to scrape what they can from the inshore grounds will wipe them out altogether. Going farther out as they have to do now is giving the inshore areas a chance to lie quiet and build up again as a feeding and breeding area for the fish. But they can't see that. They're really a strange lot."

"I can see now why my coming has been so poorly received," Jean said, the angry, cryptic remarks all quite clear now. "They think I've come to back up your decisions on not letting them use the cove."

Hobart Weatherby's quick, shrewd eyes watched the girl closely, and Jean felt them reading her thoughts, seeing them reflected in her face. "All this has upset you," he said with quiet accuracy.

"It's just that I didn't come here to find problems and get involved in controversy," Jean said.

"Then I suggest you stay entirely clear of it, my dear," Hobart Weatherby said. "Tell anyone who speaks to you about it that the decisions are strictly mine. After all, I've been making them all these years anyway."

The solution appealed instantly to Jean. She didn't want problems and she felt herself nodding. "Yes, that's fine with me," she said, knowing she sounded selfish and uncaring.

"I think that's a sensible decision on your part," the older man said. "Just why did you come here to the house at Hawk's End all of a sudden, Miss Burroughs?" he added, his sharp eyes penetrating. That question again, she said silently. This made the third time she'd been asked it since she'd arrived.

"For personal reasons," Jean replied. "To rest, to get away from a lot of things. Certainly not to find more problems."

Bob Weatherby answered quickly. "You're too lovely to have any problems, let alone some stubborn old fishermen," he said, and Jean glanced up at his pleasant smile. "If you're going to wrestle with any problem while you're here I'd like to be it."

Jean found a smile, and Hobart Weatherby stood up as Jean rose. He took her hand in both of his. "I'll make you Bob's special assignment while you're here," he said. "Now you don't worry about a thing except your own thoughts. How long do you expect to be with us?"

"I don't know," Jean said truthfully. How fast do scars heal, she added silently. How long does it take to get to know yourself?

"Well, one day we must talk about the old place," the lawyer said as they walked to the door. "I think I ought to find some way to take it off your hands altogether. It's really not good for much."

"All right, we'll discuss it one day," Jean said and found herself outside with Bob. As he drove her back to the house, the afternoon was falling into night. He was interesting and nice to be with, yet when they reached the house, she was glad to be alone. Hobart Weatherby's question had stayed with her. He had asked it one way. Ferris Duncan had asked it in another way, and Amantha had touched upon it in a stranger way. Jean sank down onto the chair in the library, a small frown creasing her brow. Just why had she come here, to the house at Hawk's End, to this cold, bleak land dusted by arctic winds and buffeted by the sea? But this had been what she wanted, the aloneness of it, she reminded herself. But was it the aloneness or something else? She heard Ferris Duncan's biting question and her lips tightened. Had it been more than trying to find peace of mind? Had she chosen Hawk's End to punish herself? Or had Hawk's End chosen her?

Angrily Jean got to her feet. She'd always let her imagination run off at the wrong times. She walked into the living room and saw the adjoining room lighted and the long table set with one place. Amantha was there, filling a plate with slices of the roast. Eating alone was going to be one of the less pleasant sidelights here, Jean realized grimly. She was doubly glad now she'd agreed to Bob Weatherby's dinner invitation. The housekeeper left the room as Jean sat down to the table and came back only when the girl had finished. Darkness had fallen, Jean noticed, and she saw Amantha hurry the dishes into the sink and leave them to wash in the morning. Jean was in the foyer as the big woman came to the door with her coat on. "Be here in the morning," Amantha muttered, and Jean nodded silently, watching her leave. She held her questions back and turned away, going down the hallway, eerily flickering with the light from the hurricane lamp Amantha had set on the hall table. In her room, Jean latched the door and decided on a small fire instead of the hurricane lamps Amantha had left there.

At least the night would be better, Jean told herself. From the window she could see the sea, only blackness now with the waves against the beach a thin white line. There'd be no storm to make the house bend tonight, no wind to push against the old timbers until cornerposts crashed down. As Jean undressed and stretched out in the big bed, she thought about Amantha. The woman had been so certain that no animal had sent the cornerpost crashing. Perhaps she did possess a kind of folk wisdom about her, and which she no doubt made more of than it warranted. Jean stretched and half-smiled as she turned on her side. Ted's letter lay on the table, a reminder of why she had come here, and the sea was a soft, distant sound. She lay awake, thinking the thoughts she wanted to think through until sleep overtook her and her eyes closed. The few logs she'd put on the fire flickered out, and the night took over the room and the sleeping girl. Outside, the night stayed silent as a tomb, as if to make up for the fury it had shown the night before.

It was in the small hours of the dark, when morning waited impatiently, that Jean opened her eyes and felt her skin cold and wet with perspiration. Something had startled her into waking, as it had the night before, and she sat up at once. The room seemed bathed in a strange, reddish glow but as she swung out of bed it faded away at once to leave her in the blackness. But from the window she saw it, in the distance, and she hurried to the glass to peer out. There, across the vast dark of the sea, a reddish glow slowly moved through the night. It could have been a ship on fire, but the girl frowned as she peered at the light. It was the color of distant fire but with a strange, ghostly hue, an incandescence rather than the strength of flame. It moved slowly, from right to left, some three miles out, she estimated. She pressed herself against the window, ignoring the coldness of the glass through the thin nightgown she wore. The reddish glow moved on steadily until, with a startling abruptness, it faded away. Only the still blackness remained and Jean stayed at the window, waiting to see if it would reappear. Finally she turned away and went back to bed. It had been an eerie sight, and she felt herself trembling. Probably from the cold of the window, she told herself, and drawing the blanket up, she held herself still in the warmth of the bed until she fell asleep, still thinking about the strange, red glow on the night sea.

CHAPTER THREE

When she woke, the morning sun had turned the room bright yellow, and she ran to the window to peer out, wondering if there'd be a blackened hulk or a fleet of vessels searching the water. But there was only the sea, a sparkling and brilliant blue. Where the eerie glow had been, she saw the dim bulk of an island. But the fire, if it had been a fire, hadn't been on the island. It had definitely moved across the water and now, in the brightness of the clear morning, she wondered if she hadn't indeed dreamt it all. It was a wonderfully clear day, and Jean dressed hurriedly in deep blue slacks and a cream blouse. She would go down to the edge of the sea, on a flat rock, and let her thoughts float in her mind, sifting and sorting them out one by one. She heard Amantha in the kitchen as she went into the hallway, following the smell of bacon and coffee.

The housekeeper in her uniform of black dress and gray apron, put a plate of bacon on the table with a letter alongside it. Jean chuckled as she saw the handwriting. Ted was keeping his word about writing every day. She put it in the pocket of her slacks to read down at the water's edge. Amantha, pail and mop in her hand, was starting from the kitchen when Jean called to her.

"I saw something strange last night," she said. "A glowing, reddish light moving across the water. Did you see it? Do you know what it might have been?"

"I saw it," the woman said, her face impassive.

"Then I didn't dream it," Jean said. "I was wondering if I had."

"You didn't dream it," the woman said, turning and hurrying from the room. Jean started to call after her but didn't. Amantha Colburn was a strange person, she concluded. Finishing her coffee, she went outside, shaking herself loose of the closed, oppressive feeling the old house seemed to wrap around her.

She clambered down from the top of the rocks, finding them a lot steeper than she had when she climbed up them the day before. Reaching the bottom where the sea curled lazily over the rocks and the tide was high, she saw a long, flat stone a dozen yards up from where she'd descended. Clambering over the wet rocks at the edge of the water, she reached the stone and sat down on it. She could see down the shoreline to the beach and beyond it to the windswept trees forever bent in self-protection. To the north she could see the end of the land, the point of the big, deep-water cove, her cove, and in front of her, the vastness of the Atlantic spread out. The low shape of the island she'd seen from her window, blue gray in the sun, was clearly visible now. Behind her the old house was out of sight, and all she could see were the big boulders that rose up to the land above. She took the letter from her pocket and read it eagerly.

Dear Jeanie girl:

Look here, another message from the outside world of pleasure-loving philistines. Thought of you when I went to the Mozart program at Fenway last night. You were always such fun to go to Mozart with, especially *Don Giovanni,* but then it's always fun to watch someone thoroughly enjoy themselves.

Don't even ask who I was with. She had a polite, refined appreciation of Mozart, and you know, what I think of polite, refined appreciation. It's like making love with gloves on. Damn little of it gets through. But then, they can't all be like you.

> You better meditate, Jeanie. That's why you fled up there. How are things coming in the self-discovery department? Meanwhile, back at the ranch, Ted's just finished a six-page fashion spread full of long sleek cars with cute little wheels and long sleek girls with cute little busts. Oh, how I wish you'd get back here. Take care.
>
> Love,
> Ted

She put the letter in her pocket, and a soft smile played across her face. Ted spoke of the hurting things only in his own, oblique way, just enough to remind her, and she was grateful to him for that. But, then, she'd been grateful to Ted for a lot of things, mostly the use of his shoulder to cry on. If he had but a small part of Ferris Duncan's inner strength Ted would be a wonderful person, she mused. She was still letting thoughts idle in her mind when she heard the sudden, sharp noise, like that of a small thunderclap. She looked up, startled, and then the sharp sound was followed by a low rumble and she felt the rock tremble. Jean looked up behind her to see the boulders at the top of the steep incline starting to topple. In seconds they were thunderously crashing onto one another, sending others to crash down in a sudden rock slide. The huge rocks gathered speed with terrifying intensity, now a swath of them, rolling and crashing down atop each other, heading toward her. She started to jump to her feet, slipped and fell to one knee and pulled herself up. There was no time left to run and no place to run to as the boulders had fanned out and were cascading down on both sides of her. Any of them could kill her, and she saw a huge one looming up above her as it bounced off a stone with a thunderous impact. Jean turned and dived into the sea just as the first of them smashed into the water alongside her.

A wave hurrying to break against the rocks caught her and threw her back into the churning, splashing maelstrom of boulders crashing into the sea. She felt herself lifted on a column of water, thrown into the air, and smashed down again. Arms flailing, she fought to swim forward, away from the boulders that crashed into the water all around her. A huge spiral of water seized and flung her sideways and she felt the glancing blow of the boulder that fell. Pain shot through her body and the world was spinning. Another rock struck her, grazing her shoulders, and the jarring impact of it sent her flipping backward in the water. She felt darkness closing in over her and tried to turn over. Drift, she commanded herself, but nothing responded and she felt a terrible weakness flooding over her. Her shoulder hurt and her head pained, the pain the only thing still keeping her from lapsing into unconsciousness, and now that began to fail as she felt her eyes closing against her will. She went under and surfaced again as the sea lifted her. She was hardly conscious now, and then something was holding her, and she was being pulled upward. She felt air against her face and she shook her head to clear it. The veil lifted from her eyes for a brief instant, and dimly she saw the side of a boat and a figure pulling her in. Then she fell unconscious.

The warmth was the first thing she felt when she woke, the warmth of another human body, holding her close. Opening her eyes, she saw she had her head against someone's chest, and as she looked up a face began to take shape, then powerful shoulders. Slowly Ferris Duncan came into view, his rugged head peering down at her, concern in his eyes. The soft throb of an outboard motor told her she was in the big dory, and she managed a smile of reassurance and gratitude. She stayed still, unwilling to leave the comfortable circle of his arms.

"You saved my life," she murmured.

"No, you did that when you dived into the water," Ferris answered. "I was coming up the shoreline when I heard the sounds and saw you dive in."

"I was going under when you came," Jean said. "You did the saving. I'll never be able to thank you enough."

He reached out to take the tiller of the boat and correct their course, and she was sorry to leave the security of those powerful arms. Following his gaze, she looked back at the rocks where only a relatively small trail of dislodged stones marked the spot.

"What did it, Ferris?" Jean asked, sitting up straighter, glad for the warmth of the sun that shone on her wet clothes.

"I don't know," the man said. "I've never known them to shake loose like that. An underground tremor, maybe, possibly down on the ocean floor. It probably sent a shock wave up that hit right at that spot."

"I'm glad it was you who came along," Jean said. "I wanted to see you, to talk to you."

"Wait till I get to shore," Ferris said, and she saw he had turned the nose of the boat in toward a small inlet, not more than a little circle of sand indented on the shoreline with a few trees hanging low to the water from a ledge of soil. She also saw the old man standing there and, as they nosed onto the sand, the frown on his parchment-skin weathered face. Ferris swung from the boat, quickly telling Enoch what had happened. He reached up and lifted Jean down to the ground and she felt his strength as his big hands held her. On the ground, she looked up as Ferris turned to the old man whose eyes still held that angry blaze she'd seen at their first meeting.

"And you went and saved her, did you," Enoch spat out, his words directed at Ferris, his eyes boring into the girl. Jean's temper rocketed at once, and holding the old man's bitter eyes, she answered.

"I think your friend Enoch would rather you'd let the sea or the rocks take care of me, Ferris," she said. She glared at the stern-faced, bitter old man. "At least you've the honesty not to deny it," she added.

"That's right," Enoch threw back at her, and, with a motion as swift and sure as Ferris's, he vaulted into the dory. "You coming?" he said to Ferris Duncan.

"No, I'll walk back. You take the boat in," Ferris said, putting his shoulder to the prow of the dory and pushing her off the sand. Enoch rowed a few feet farther out, his eyes still glaring, and then turned the dory around. The blast of the outboard as he sent the craft leaping forward was an angry curse back at them.

Jean suddenly felt her legs trembling and she sank down on the sand of the tiny inlet. "He really hates me, doesn't he?" she murmured.

"He's no worse than the others," Ferris said. "It's not you, really, it's what you stand for, what you mean to them, to all of us."

"You mean the right to fish the cove," Jean said. "I met with Hobart Weatherby yesterday."

"And his son?"

"Yes, Bob was there," Jean answered.

"He's no better than the old man," Ferris Duncan said, and she was surprised at the cold anger in his voice.

"I can understand how you feel, Ferris, how all the others feel," Jean began, but he interrupted her angrily.

"No, you can't," he cut in. "It goes deeper down than you've any idea. They've always blamed old Weatherby. He was here to blame, but now you're here and they can turn on you."

"But I've never bothered with the place," Jean protested.

"All the same, Weatherby's been acting for somebody. That's all they know. If you didn't exist, then Weatherby wouldn't have the right to keep us from fishing the cove, least not till a new owner took the place."

"And that's not too likely to happen," Jean said and saw Ferris nod in agreement.

"There'd be no talk from Weatherby about it being private property and him acting for the owner because there'd be no owner."

"Of course, there'd be my estate and that's legal to act for, or the same for anyone else who owned the place," Jean said.

"It wouldn't be the same, not to folks around here. They figure it simpler. No owner exists, then it's free to fish the cove."

"Are you trying to warn me, Ferris?" Jean asked.

"I'm trying to tell you how folks think here."

"Hobart Weatherby says you've brought your troubles on yourselves," she said. She watched the hardness come into Ferris's eyes as she went on to tell him exactly what the lawyer had said. When she finished, his eyes were of onyx, and the line of his jaw tight.

"Those are lies," he said to her. "There's been no overfishing at all. It's just that we're caught in one of those cycles that happens with fish, and with many animals, from time to time. We want to fish the cove until the fish go back to the shore areas in large numbers, and they will, soon as this cycle and whatever's caused it has run its course. Maybe there's been a change in the sea bottom along the shore that's disturbed them. Maybe the food there is low. It could be any number of things but it's not anything we've done."

Jean studied the intensity of the big man's handsome face. He could be wrong but he wasn't lying, she felt, not deliberately, not consciously. But people often lie to themselves, too, she knew.

"Weatherby talks of it from the four walls of his warm office," Ferris threw out at her. "But it's not just our livelihood, it's our lives that are at stake."

"How do you mean that, Ferris?" Jean asked.

"To get to good fishing grounds now, we've got to go ten to fifteen miles north and out from here," Ferris answered. "Do you know how many men have died because of that in the last year alone? Do you know what that means? In these waters the storms come up fast. Three or four hours from shore means the difference in getting back safely or being caught in a storm. And in the spring, when the icebergs come down from the north, we're in their path and it's bad, real bad, especially in the early morning fogs."

There was a powerful vibrancy in Ferris Duncan's anger. Jean remembered that Bob Weatherby had said that the fishermen needed only to go out a little farther to find their fishing grounds, but Ferris had given her a very different picture of what that meant. She had told the Weatherbys she'd stay out of it and, more importantly, had promised herself that. But now Ferris's strong, heartfelt words were impossible to just push aside.

"Let me speak to Hobart Weatherby again," she said.

"It's your land, isn't it?" the big man retorted. "For you to do with as you want."

"Yes and no," Jean said. "Technically it's mine, but actually I might just as well be a visitor here. I don't know anything about these things. I don't know the right thing to do, and I'm honest enough to admit that. But I promise you I'll speak to Hobart Weatherby again. Tell the others that and give me a little more time."

"They've little mood for time, I can tell you that," Ferris said.

"And I've little taste for this," Jean said. "I didn't come here to get involved in more problems."

"What did send you here, Jean Burroughs?" the big man asked, his voice suddenly soft. "Tell me what it was. Tell me what makes a rose try to find a place for itself in a stone?"

Jean sat back, feeling the wetness of her blouse clinging to her breasts, revealing every line and point of them as she leaned upon her elbow in the sand. She watched Ferris Duncan's eyes rove across her figure, and there was a kindness in them she hadn't seen before. She suddenly wanted to borrow strength from this rugged man, to tell him everything, and to draw upon the silent, inner power that was his. His quiet questions smoothed her way, and she heard herself telling him of things old and new and those too long held inside herself.

"What did you do wherever you came from?" he asked her.

"I was a buyer for a large dress house," Jean said. "I'd a good salary and a good job. My mother died when I was very young, and my father saw to it that I was sent to all the best schools and given the best of everything. I guess you'd say I've been a fortunate young woman."

"I would," Ferris Duncan said quietly.

"I was part of a swinging set. We lived on the martini-and-weekend-party circuit," Jean said, and she paused as she scanned Ferris Duncan's face. "I suppose that's all so far from your world that you don't even understand what I'm talking about," she went on. "It's a life where the most important thing is having fun and filling up every spare moment with something new, something different, only nothing is ever really that new or that different. But, good or bad, it was fun in its own kind of way. The crowd kept changing, old ones would leave and new ones join. Then Evan Reed came into our group."

Jean paused again to meet Ferris's steady gaze and then, drawing a deeper breath, she went on. "Evan and I had an affair. It wasn't the first for me, and I doubt it was the first for him. But it was the first time he'd ever really fallen in love. I should have known better than to let him. I know that now. Evan was different than the others, sweeter, gentler, a softer person. Maybe that's what drew me to him. But I never loved him, not really, certainly not the way he loved me. I think now I've never known what love is, the real thing, that is. I've had mad crushes and infatuations and what I thought was love. But I'd never really thought much about the real meaning of love, about the pricelessness of it, about what it gives to you and what it asks of you, the privileges of being loved and the responsibilities of it. But Evan taught me."

"How?" Ferris asked softly.

"He killed himself," Jean said flatly. There was only a flicker of expression in Ferris's big, strong face.

"He found me with someone else," Jean continued. "That was bad enough, but later I told him I'd never been really in love with him. He begged me to give it another try. He said if I did, I'd see things his way. I never would have, I knew that, and I refused.

I don't think I was too understanding, either. It was over, and I just wanted nothing more of it. I didn't want to think about those things that I know now must be a part of every relationship."

As she spoke, the rugged man before her faded away, and the sea behind him became a gray haze. She saw herself alone in a room with a soft-eyed young man, his face quietly desperate as he tried to reach someone who wouldn't be reached, a girl all of surface callousness.

"You took what I brought you, Jean," he was saying. "You shouldn't have, then."

"Maybe not," the girl was saying. "I never gave it that much thought."

"I gave you a gift, Jean, not something to kick away, to walk over. I love you. That's enough to make it work. Just give it a chance," the young man was answering. But the girl was shaking her head and having none of a onesided love, knowing that much, if little else, about love.

Then the scene faded away as quickly as it had appeared before her, and Jean saw Ferris Duncan there, waiting for her to go on.

"Evan killed himself a few days later," she said quietly. "I still have the letter he left me. I came apart then. All that it meant hit me and made me see everything I was and everything I wasn't. I tried living as if it had been no more than a sorry incident, putting all the blame on poor Evan, making him into the weak one. Yes, he was weak, but that wasn't enough. I tried to see my way past myself, and it didn't work. I couldn't escape my own part in it. Finally, I knew I had to get away by myself where I could think out all the things that had stirred to life inside me. I had to find the meaning of living and make some sense out of a world I saw with new eyes. Oh, it's all mixed up inside me yet, but it'll sort itself out. I know it will."

"And you came here," Ferris concluded, and she saw him frown, his eyes deep, troubled. "Why here to Hawk's End?" he asked. "I'd think there'd be a lot of better places for you to go off by yourself than this hard land and that old wreck of a house."

Jean shrugged. "I didn't know the house was what it is and it just seemed a convenient place to come," she said. His eyes were still troubled, the frown still on his face as he gazed at her. She wasn't going to tell him about sitting up in the dead of night and knowing she had to come here to the house at Hawk's End. She'd revealed enough that was private and painful without adding strange impulses that would make her look foolish as well.

"I guess I should be glad of one thing," she went on. "It showed I can feel, I can be shaken and hurt. I'm not that empty or that callous inside. Those who could shake something like that off are the sorry ones."

"Yes, I'd say you were right there," Ferris commented, and she met his deep, black brown eyes. His hand took her by the shoulder, firm yet surprisingly gentle. "You've thinking to do, all right," he said. "Maybe more than you know. Enough in any case."

His rugged face was just above hers, and Jean felt her lips part as she leaned forward, reaching up to his face. His kiss was soft but only for an instant, and then he gathered her into his arms and she felt the power of this man, and she liked the hardness of his kiss as he pressed her mouth open. When he drew back, his eyes were deep pools of black fire, but his face remained unsmiling and he said nothing.

"Let's say that was a thank you for saving my life," she finally breathed. "Not much of one, but it'll have to do for the moment."

She almost said *don't* as he took his arms from around her and left her feeling unprotected. Instead, she reached up and put her hand on his powerful chest.

"And thanks for listening," she half-whispered. He pulled her to her feet.

"I've got to get back. I'll see you to the house," he said, starting off. "I know a shorter way there."

Jean fell in beside him, finding his hand with hers, wanting the protectiveness of it. The tiny inlet was surrounded by sharply inclined walls of rock and scrubby brush but he led her up a narrow, steep passageway. They had to move single file on it and he went back of her, holding her shoulder with one hand as the passage rose sharply and she saw the sea below. It leveled off, widening, and she paused to look out at the distant shape of the island a few miles away. She thought of mentioning the strange reddish glow she'd seen in the night and then decided against it. Instead, she nodded her head toward the sea as they paused.

"What island is that out there, Ferris?" she inquired.

"Rock Island, it's called," he answered.

"Is it used for anything?"

"No one goes there, not from here, anyway. No one in a hundred years has set foot on it," he said. Her eyes asked the question of him and he went on. "It's called a bad-luck place," he said. "Folks that live by the sea live with danger enough. They don't add to it by ignoring what others have lived by, whether it's legend or superstition. It's a bad-luck place with a bad history. Besides, it's no good for anything. It's all rock and a few old trees. In a heavy storm the sea sweeps right over it."

Jean gazed out at the dim shape a moment longer, seeing the strange glow again in her mind, and then Ferris was moving on, and she hurried after him. At a ledge of rock separated from the next one he swung her across with easy grace, and she felt her breasts brush against his chest as he held her close. The other side of the ledge led down to the beach, and when they reached the sand he halted, his hand on her arm.

"I'll do my best with the others," he said. Unexpectedly he touched her cheek with his big hand, rubbing the back of it along the smoothness of her face. "You've beauty enough to make a man forget everything," he murmured, and then he was gone, climbing back along the passageway over the ledge, and she hurried along the beach. As she neared the end of the sand, she crossed up to the dune road. Climbing up the rocks was not for her, not this soon, and she shuddered as she saw where death had come so close to her. Her shoulder twinged in pain as an added reminder. It was the second time in as many days that death had brushed her, and as with the cornerpost, she had been miraculously lucky. The house was before her now, and it seemed to lean forward as she came to it, as though it would embrace her with its shattered shingles and hanging boards.

Amantha Colburn was crossing the hallway as Jean entered and the woman halted, taking in the girl's still half-wet and wrinkled clothes.

"I had to dive into the sea," Jean said, walking down the hallway. "I was almost killed."

The woman's face was unchanged, but Jean saw the sharp flicker of her eyes as she stood waiting to hear more.

"I was sitting by the water when it happened," Jean explained. "An entire line of boulders started to shake loose. They crashed down from the very top of the rocks. I would have been crushed to death if I hadn't dived into the water. A fisherman, Ferris Duncan, pulled me out. The rockslide must have been caused by an earth tremor of some sort, perhaps even on the ocean floor."

Jean saw a fright in the big woman's eyes, there for an instant and then gone.

"No, no earth tremor," Amantha Colburn said. "No earth tremor anywhere."

The woman turned away abruptly, moving into the kitchen. Jean followed her, watching the woman's broad back. It was the same manner she had used about the cornerpost, adamantly saying it had been no animal. And she had been right, Jean reminded herself grimly.

"Amantha, why do you say it was no earth tremor?" Jean asked from the doorway, watching the woman's face intently, watching for some answer that might reveal itself in a glance, a brief expression. But the woman's face remained carved of wood. "What makes you so certain. Amantha?" Jean prodded.

"I know, that's all," the woman said flatly.

"They just took that moment to come loose?" Jean said. "One of those strange things that happen? Coincidence, fate, is that it?"

"Maybe. Maybe something like that."

"That's all you have to say?"

"That's all."

The woman, mop in hand, turned away and left the room. Jean bit her lower lip in anger. The big, gaunt woman could irritate with her manner, but there was something beyond mere secretiveness in it. In her was a wisdom more felt than revealed. Jean walked into the hall, started for her room, and paused beside the chair next to the hall closet. Amantha's coat lay on the chair and a book on top of it. Jean reached down to pick up the book as the title blazed out at her, and her lips formed the words noiselessly: *Realities of the Occult.* Opening the book, she read from it and a frown deepened on her brow. Certain passages were underlined, paragraphs marked, and after a few moments she closed the book and went into the library where she heard Amantha stirring about. Jean placed the book on the table where the housekeeper was cleaning, and the woman paused for an instant and went on working.

"Amantha, when I arrived here you said I was here because I had to come," Jean said. "Why did you say that?"

The woman halted her work to look at the girl, and Jean thought she saw her eyes lose some of their stoniness. Amantha's gaze was steady, penetrating, and Jean, frowning, asked again. "Why do you say I had to come here?" she questioned.

"Because it's true," the woman said finally. "Because you could do nothing else."

Amantha Colburn spoke quietly, firmly, making it sound as though it were but a simple statement of fact.

"Why couldn't I do anything else?" Jean pressed.

"Because you are possessed," the woman answered softly. "Possessed."

The answer, softly given, struck with a force that was out of proportion in its startlingness and Jean felt the frown that creased her forehead. "Why, that's absolutely ridiculous, Amantha," Jean said. "Surely, you don't really believe in such things."

The woman's stare was unyielding. "You came because you had to come," she repeated.

"Nonsense!" Jean shot back. "I came because I wanted to. I wanted to get away, to be alone in a quiet place."

"Why here, to Hawk's End?" Amantha prodded, and Jean snapped out the answer she'd given the others. "Because the house is mine, it was left to me. It fitted just what I wanted," she said. "It was logical and convenient."

"You came because you were called," the woman said in her flat, certain voice.

Jean felt her face flush, felt her hands clench, and she saw herself again sitting up in bed that moonless night, waking out of a sound sleep, hearing a name, yes, a call.

"No, that's preposterous," she answered and heard the quiver in her voice. "If I'm possessed who or what is possessing me?" she asked.

"Another soul, another spirit. An astral body," the woman said. "Someone who has waited for you."

Jean swallowed and felt the tightness in her throat, and she walked across the room, opening her hands, which had clenched themselves tightly again.

"This is absolutely ridiculous," she said.

"Only to those who are afraid to know about the other world, who are afraid to recognize it exists," the housekeeper said. "But it exists, even though we can't explain it. It still exists. It's just as real as the world we can touch. Today we even admit to part of it and close our eyes to the rest, and we give the part we admit a lot of fancy names."

"You mean extrasensory perception," Jean said. Amantha nodded. "Yes, and it exists. It's as real as the stones and the trees."

"Yes, extrasensory perception is generally recognized as an existing phenomenon, though we don't understand how it operates. And some people are specially gifted with it. But that doesn't mean that every kind of foolishness has to be accepted."

"You think that reaching another person is so much nonsense? You think possession is ridiculous? Just look around you, think of the things you've known. People reach each other without a word being spoken or written, without even a sound. Everybody who can feel knows that. You go into a room and there's maybe one person there who reaches out to you right away, one person you make contact with, and you do it through the force of your inner being. You've not touched anyone, not spoken, and yet you've been drawn to one person you never knew before."

Jean said nothing, but she knew the truth of the woman's words. She'd experienced that often enough and had wondered idly about it herself. Electric, magnetic, chemical attraction were some of the names she'd heard given to that. But maybe they were all groping attempts to explain something beyond explaining.

"But possession, a spirit or a force possessing another person's emotions and mind, that's straight out of witchcraft," Jean said.

"Is it?" the woman answered. "No, it's straight out of life. It happens all the time and we just give it other names. We don't like the word *possession.* It frightens us, but it's around us all the time. People kill and rape and torture and commit every kind of crime because they're possessed, ruled by the powers of darkness, an evil force that holds them in its grip. We call what they do hate, sometimes insanity, but they're possessed. They're possessed by a force that destroys their will, their reason. How often does a killer tell his questioners that he didn't know why he killed, that he just had to do it?

"And sometimes, we call it love. People can be possessed by love, too. Did you ever know someone so in love they can't think of anything but the person they love? That person fills their every moment so that nothing else exists for them, no one else, nothing else. They're possessed, too."

"Yes, I've known of that," Jean said, hearing the tightness in her voice.

"Yes, we're possessed, no matter what we like to call it. We're possessed by forces we know and forces we don't know. Sometimes we can touch them and see them, and we know who they are, and we can fight them off. But there are the others, the ones we can't touch or see. They speak to us, too. They command us, from beyond the grave, from anywhere. They seek and they seek till they find the one they must have."

"No, it's not so, not the way you mean it," Jean said, and she saw the woman shrug and regard her with an uncompromising stare.

"You'll know," she said. "Or maybe you know already. You've just refused to admit it."

She picked up the book and strode from the room, pausing in the doorway. "I won't be in tomorrow. Not the next day, either. I've things to do," she said. "There's food in the icebox, enough till I come back."

Jean stayed in the library and listened to Amantha put away her cleaning things and leave. She waited a moment more and then went to her room, drawing a bath, reminding herself that Bob Weatherby would be arriving to take her to dinner. It would be more welcome than ever now. Amantha's talk of being possessed was ridiculous, of course, and yet she had been terribly shaken by it. In the woman's wild talk were kernels of truth that clung with their own, stubborn persistence. Amantha Colburn had spoken of strange forces, of astral bodies, of possession, but there had been more, not put into words, questions that cried out for truth. Others had asked them of her and she'd given answers, while deep inside her she knew those answers were less than true. Why had she come here to the house at Hawk's End, they'd asked, and now as she undressed, she asked it again of herself. Why hadn't she chosen to go to Cape Cod, where she'd spent so many summers? The Wilson's cottage was hers anytime she wanted it, and she had often used it after the regular season was over. Why hadn't she gone to the quietness of Lakeview in the Berkshires, where she'd spent many a Christmas? Why, on that night when she'd wakened in her apartment, hadn't any of those names come to her? Why had the house at Hawk's End reverberated in her mind as she sat naked in bed, commanding, insistent, a place she'd never been, a place whose existence she'd virtually forgotten?

She had told herself she hungered for the hard, uncompromising bleakness of this land. But had that really been so? Or was that but another reason she had supplied for something she couldn't explain and hadn't wanted to think that much about. As she bathed she thought about the rock slide and the cornerpost, how death had come within a fraction of an inch. Was that part of being possessed? The very word was medieval and made her shudder, and she was angry at herself for letting Amantha leave without questioning her further. Cryptic statements always bothered her, and the woman's strange Dark Ages ideas were tenacious and left a cold knot in the pit of her stomach. She angrily pushed them aside and concentrated on dressing. She put on a deep blue dress with a high bodice that was both modest and provocative. The day was sliding away as she stood by the window and watched the lavender and pink of the sky join the sea at the horizon line. Bob wasn't due for another half hour, and she wanted something to keep her mind from dwelling on Amantha and her strange ideas. Diving into her purse as the thought burst on her, she came up with a pen and a pad of note-paper. Ted deserved a letter in return, if only a short one. She sat down at the table and began to write. She wrote quickly, telling him everything that had happened and including Amantha's remarks, keeping it all light and humorous. As she sealed the envelope, she saw the headlights of the car approaching, and slipping on a coat, she went outside to meet Bob. His eyes reflected his appreciation of her loveliness, and they drove back along the coast for at least an hour and then, turning inland, he drew up before a stately carriage house that had become a restaurant. She dropped the letter in a mailbox there.

Bob Weatherby was the very opposite of this unyielding, humorless land. He was attentive, talkative, interested, and he'd a way of asking questions that elicited a lot of information. Jean wanted to make it an evening of carefree conversation and she tried, but she never freed herself from the things that crowded in on her, and over dinner she heard herself telling Bob everything that had happened, from the rock slide through Amantha's accusation to the incident with the cornerpost. His eyes were narrowed when she finished, as though he were juggling a variety of thoughts at once.

"You know, Jean," he began slowly, "I'd like to see you stay here at Hawk's End for obvious reasons, all selfish ones, naturally. But maybe this just isn't the place for you. Maybe you ought to go somewhere else to get away from whatever it is you're getting away from."

Jean wondered if he noticed her lips open at once and her struggle to hold back the words that almost tumbled from them. No, I can't leave, she had almost said in instant answer. It was as though someone else had tried to answer for her, someone—or something. Of course, she could go somewhere else to be alone. Why had she immediately tried to refuse? Bob was going on, and she was glad he couldn't see her hands, clenched tightly in her lap.

"In view of the business with the fishing rights and all that unpleasantness, you might just be adding to your tensions instead of relaxing," he said. "Father would handle things, as he always has, and you could come back someday when it's all settled down."

He was making sense, Jean knew, but the whole thought of leaving was out of the question, and she wondered why it was so unthinkable. She'd not found the quiet solitude she sought here, not yet anyway, but she had found a kind of rugged strength. Perhaps that was it, she told herself and hurriedly went on with questions of her own.

"Where did your father get Amantha Colburn?" she asked. "She told me she doesn't mix with the townspeople."

"She's done some housework for us," Bob answered. "And she was the only one we could get on short notice. She lives up on the hill directly east of the house, alone in a place tucked in among the rocks at the very top. She's pretty much a recluse."

"The wives of the fishermen ought to have welcomed the chance for a little extra money, I should have thought," Jean said. "Why won't any of them go to the house? And why won't anyone set foot on Rock Island?"

Bob's laugh was slow and easy and more of a deep chuckle than anything else. "I see you've been listening to them," he said. "They're full of old wives' tales and legends. In the worst of the winter that's all they do, sit around and tell tall stories and embroider old legends. I don't know what keeps them from Rock Island, or the house, and I've never cared enough to find out. Father told you they were simple people."

"Maybe so, but I've learned what going out a little further to fish means in terms of danger," Jean said. "I wonder if they shouldn't be allowed to fish the cove."

Bob Weatherby's eyes seemed to grow smaller but his genial smile stayed fixed. "I thought you'd agreed to leave that up to my father," he said, a touch of amused tolerance in his voice.

"I know I did," Jean said. "It's just that maybe there is another side to it. I want to do what's right."

"Of course you do. We all do," Bob said. "Why don't you talk to my father about it again yourself? That'd be the best thing to do. Meanwhile, you've had your share of weird happenings since you got here, and I say let's talk about anything but this place and its problems. You tell me about Boston and I'll tell you about Halifax. Now there's an uneven exchange if I ever heard one."

Jean laughed and let Bob pull her away from her own dark musings. He didn't try to find out about her life in Boston, and he never touched on what she was here to get away from, and she was grateful for that. He let her tell him whatever she wanted to tell, and he spoke of his years in Halifax with unconcealed distaste. "I guess I was used to the good things in life and wasn't cut out to be a struggling lawyer grubbing for crumbs," he said. "I'm not much of a trial lawyer anyway."

Dinner, a fragrant cheese soup and boiled lobster, ending with hot apple pie, was delicious, and by the time they drove back, she was feeling relaxed. Bob drove the winding roads expertly with one hand, holding hers with the other. But when they drove up to the black, forbidding bulk of the old house she felt its presence reach out to her instantly. Bob waited while she lighted two of the hurricane lamps and then, at the door, she felt his arms holding her.

"You sure you want to stay here alone again?" he asked.

"Why, sir, what would the good people of the village think?" she laughed and heard his soft, answering chuckle.

"I wasn't meaning that, but it's a great idea," he said. "I meant you could stay at our place."

She pressed his arm. "Thanks, but I'll be all right," she said. His arms tightened, and she felt his lips on hers, a short kiss, tender, soft, and she was sorry he didn't linger there.

"Think of what I said, Jean, about going away, for now, anyway," he said.

"I will. I promise," she answered.

She watched him wave as he drove off, and then she closed the door, latching it. She left one lighted lamp in the hallway and took the other one into her room. Bob's reminder about leaving had brought up all the things she had finally managed to push aside during dinner. Any other girl would have left after that first night. But she had stayed, and now had no thoughts of leaving. Why had she immediately rejected the thought when Bob brought it up? Jean closed off her mind. She'd not let herself be carried away into wild imaginings by an old woman's ridiculous ideas, the mumblings of an old recluse with a head full of strange thoughts. The girl shook herself angrily, as if to shake away the things that clung to her like a shroud, and she undressed quickly and slipped into the warmth of the bed. She lay there, listening to the stillness, until she finally went to sleep, forcing her mind into blankness.

But sleep was a restless, tossing thing, full of crashing rocks and thunderous boulders, and the girl's pillow grew wet with perspiration. The hour had moved toward morning when suddenly she woke, a fright in her eyes as she sat up. For a moment the room seemed bathed in pink again and then, as she swung from the bed, it went away and she raced to the window. A moon hung high in the sky and there, on the water, the reddish glow moved slowly, just about where Rock Island lay. Jean watched it, transfixed. Despite its color, it was a cold light and it moved slowly to the left until suddenly, like a candle blown out, it faded away and only the moon remained. Jean returned to the bed and held the covers tightly to her until her body stopped its trembling. She went to sleep again finally, and the night moved on in silence.

CHAPTER FOUR

The ringing wakened her, and she lay there for a moment, seeing the warm yellow of the morning sun, wondering what it was. Then she leaped from bed and clattered down the hallway and into the library where the phone kept on with its insistent ringing. She heard Bob's voice, as bright as the morning.

"How about my picking you up just before noon," he said. "I told Father what you've been thinking, and he'd like to talk to you about it."

"Fine," Jean said. "I'll be here or down at the beach. It looks like it might be warm enough for some sunbathing."

"No rocks?" he chuckled.

"No rocks," she echoed. "I'll see you later." She put down the phone, rubbed sleep from her eyes, and went back to her room. The sea sparkled outside the window, and the air was clear and clean; it was no morning for ridiculous thoughts and dark wonderings. She threw on shorts and a halter top and hurried outside, refusing to even glance back at the rocks, unwilling to think of her brush with death. This was a warm morning full of living and even the sound of the gulls was warmer and less lonely. She crossed the dune road and scrambled down one of the dunes to the beach, almost falling. She was on the sand, almost at the water, before she saw the figure there.

"Ferris," she cried in surprise. He must have been standing in back of one of the dunes, she realized, as he came toward her. "This is a nice surprise."

His smile was short but she felt the deep warmth of it. "Were you waiting to see me?" she asked, watching his eyes move across the long, slender line of her legs and up to the full swell of her breasts.

"Maybe," he said. "I wanted to see if you were all right after yesterday."

"Yes, I bounce back quickly," she answered. "Can you stay awhile?"

He shook his head. "Enoch's waiting in town for me," he said. "We're taking the dory and trying some inshore spots down the way, not that we expect much luck."

Jean sat down on the firm, white sand and felt the big man's eyes on her. As she stretched out she saw him squat down beside her, a slow smile touching his lips.

"I'll take a minute more," he said, and she knew that by staying the "minute more" he was saying all the things most men say with words.

"Thank you, Ferris," she said quietly, her eyes tracing the line of his strong face. "I told you about myself yesterday. What about you? Have you always lived here?"

"Yes. And my father and his father before him," he said.

"Where do you live?" she asked.

"The street that goes along the harbor front, along the seawall. I've a nice place with my aunt there. The last house on the street."

"No girls?" she queried.

"There've been some," he said. "None like you though, not even the prettiest of them." He gazed out to sea, seemingly embarrassed at having compared her to the others. She touched his arm, lightly, with her hand. "Have you ever thought about leaving here?" she asked. "About doing something else?"

"Once in a while," he said. "Maybe I would if I had someone to do it for. Alone, there's no need. But I'd have to be somewhere near the sea."

"I'm sure of that," Jean smiled, and he stood up abruptly. "I've got to go," he said. "I'll speak to the others. They won't believe you, but they might wait a little longer."

"Good," she answered. "I'm going to see Hobart Weatherby later this morning. I'll have more to tell you afterward."

"Enoch and I will sail up here in the afternoon," Ferris Duncan said. "We'll pull onto the beach. If you're back, come down."

"I will," she said. She watched him go up the sand dunes in easy, springing bounds, and then she stretched out on the sand and let the sun caress her. She'd almost asked Ferris if he believed in legends, but she had decided not to spoil the moment. Closing her eyes, she listened to the sound of the sea against the sand and the cries of the seabirds. The wind blew steadily, but the sun took the edge from it. By afternoon, though, there'd be no more sunbathing, she knew. This was indeed a land where one had to seize the moments of pleasure it grudgingly gave. She lay there for a little more than an hour and then she sat up, squinting her eyes across the water to where she could just make out the line of Rock Island. A small frown creased her brow and a thought gathered strength in her mind. Getting to her feet, she hurried back to the house and changed into a simple shirtwaist of deep pink. She lay a heavy gray sweater on the chair to take with her.

She never thought Amantha Colburn was a person she could miss, but she did. The house was silent as a tomb, and as she went into the hallway after changing, she saw the letter stuck into the slot of the door. The postman had come and gone, by bicycle probably, without her hearing him. Of course, Ted hadn't gotten her letter yet when this one was written, and she thought in amusement of what kind of reply it would bring. She stood by the library window and opened the envelope.

Jeanie girl:

Just a shortie this time, but a letter's a letter. Very busy day. Tonight I'll be shooting late on a special issue. While you're concerned with the philosophy of life I'll be concerned with the perspiration of it.

But that's the way of things. There are queen bees and there are drones.

Love,
your favorite drone,
T.

She glanced out the window and saw Bob's car approaching. She put away the note and was outside when he pulled to a halt, his face wreathed in smiles.

"You're happy this morning," she commented.

"Why not?" he said. "How often do I get to pick up a pretty girl around here?"

She slid into the car beside him and smiled up at his affable geniality. After any time spent with Ferris, other men had to seem shallow, superficial, if not weak. But Bob Weatherby's open eagerness held its own brand of charm, and she settled back in the car.

"Can't say that you're terribly bright-eyed this morning," he commented.

"I'm still bothered by the things that have been said and have happened," she replied. "It's foolish of me, but it's a vulnerable period for me, I guess."

"Someday I'd like to hear about what you had to get away from," Bob said.

"Someday," she agreed and thought of how Ferris Duncan's silent strength had drawn the truth from her as a magnet draws metal to itself. When they reached the white, frame office in town, Hobart Weatherby was at the door and showed Jean into his private office.

"Bob tells me you've been listening to some of our more persuasive fishermen," he laughed.

"I did get another picture of what this means to them," Jean said. "It made me wonder about what was the right thing to do. I told Bob that."

"Yes, my dear," the lawyer nodded, his tall frame straight, his sharp eyes intent. "That's the most important thing of all, to do what's right, for everyone concerned. I've taken some steps to assure us both about that. I've contacted the Canadian government's Bureau of Fish and Game, Coastal Waters Division. They keep scientific records of the life patterns of all species of fish. I discussed the matters of breeding and food cycles of the coastal species in these waters and asked them for a special report. The report is being readied for me."

Hobart Weatherby paused, and Jean saw him probe her eyes, and then a faint smile crossed his face. "I see you're ahead of me, already, Miss Burroughs," he said. "And you're completely right. If the report tells us that the cycle is considered near an end, then we can agree to let them fish the cove without fear of depletion because the fish will be returning to their normal coastal waters. However, if the cycle is of still undetermined length, according to government studies, then that puts a different picture on things. You can still open the cove to fishing but at least you'll have proper information to back up your decision. Everyone, including the fishermen, will have something concrete to go on."

"That's a wonderful approach," Jean said happily. Hobart Weatherby beamed at her as she rose, Bob at her side.

"Then everything will stay as is until the report is in our hands," Hobart Weatherby said, and Jean nodded. As she rose to go, a small moment of uncertainty stirred within her, and she paused, Bob at her side, turning to the older man.

"I think this is the right thing," she said. "I hope so. In any case, if the government report is unfavorable, I want to open the cove to fishing at once."

"Let's cross that one when we come to it," the lawyer smiled, and Bob guided Jean out of the office.

"Father has the people's best interests at heart," Bob said as they got into the car. "He always has, even though they can't see it half the time."

As the car cleared the town's line of wooden houses, Jean refused Bob's invitation for lunch, quickly putting her hand on his arm as his face crumpled. "It's just that I want to spend more time by myself, especially today," she said. "I guess I'm still upset, and when we go out again I want to be able to enjoy it."

"I'll take a rain check," he said, brightening.

"You have it," she said as they drove back toward the house. She saw the rocky hill beyond, rising up to the center of the land, sparse vegetation clinging to the rocks.

"Is that where Amantha lives, up there?" she asked, and Bob nodded.

"There's a narrow footpath up," he said. "I've never been there, but my father has."

They drove up to the house, and she got out, letting Bob's hand hold hers for an extra moment. His eyes were filled with concern. "Let me help you, Jean," he said. "Anything you want, anywhere you want to go, just tell me."

"Is there a place to rent a boat near here, a small outboard?" Jean asked and saw the frown cross Bob's face.

"Yes, Hank Thompson's at the end of town," he said. "But why would you want a boat?"

"I like to sail," Jean said blandly, unwilling to give voice to the thought lodged in the back of her mind, not yet anyway. "I did it every year at Cape Cod and I thought it'd be nice to do some while I'm here."

Bob shrugged. "Whenever you want, I'll take you down to Hank," he said. She squeezed his hand and stepped back.

"Call me tomorrow," she said. "And thank your father again for me." Bob waved at her and drove away. Though she knew it was too early for Ferris to appear, she cast a glance at the beach before going into the house. Inside, the silence of the old house closed around her at once. She paused at the foot of the stairway and gazed up at the new wood rail where the cornerpost had been. She turned and started up the stairway, Amantha's words ringing in her ears even as she denied any truth in them. The dust on the second-floor landing was now scattered and imprinted by the marks of the man who had fixed the balustrade, but she recalled how it had been smooth and undisturbed that morning when she went up to look at it. Moving down the long hallway of the second floor, her footsteps left a trail in the dust there as she pushed open the door of the first room. It had been a second-floor parlor, she saw, and the faded curtains were still hanging, the scattered old chairs looking like old men waiting for death. She moved on to the next room and found this one had once been covered by protective sheets that were, for the most part, half-off the small table and the few chairs and the bureau. A crystal vase stood on the bureau with a kind of defiant pride. Jean closed the door and went on.

The last room of the hallway opened a few feet this side of the tree trunk that lay smashed against the rear of the house. The door, warped and sagging, opened reluctantly, and Jean had to use all her strength to pry it wide enough to enter. The room was a bedroom, and she saw the open closet against one wall, rows of long dresses hanging in it. A dusty, cherrywood dresser stood against the opposite wall, and she went into the room, feeling the clammy, musty dampness of it. The old dresses almost fell apart at her touch as she let her fingers move over them. Then she turned to the dresser. An old silver-backed mirror and a brush lay atop it, and opening the first drawer, she saw two combs, a small powder box, and rusted hairclips. The second drawer held nightgowns and petticoats, a pair of slippers and a long robe, deep pink with blue edging. The last drawer held a shawl and atop it, a faded daguerreotype in a shattered glass frame. As she picked it up the glass fell from it, and she peered at the faint picture, not certain if it was an early daguerreotype or a colored drawing. But it was a girl, strong-featured with long hair, an arresting more than a pretty face. Jean stared at the picture and felt herself drawn to it, as though it were of someone she knew. Finally she put the picture back and closed the drawer. A woman had lived here in the house at Hawk's End, more than a hundred years ago. Who was she, Jean wondered, and again she thought of Amantha Colburn. The big, gaunt woman would know, she was certain.

Closing the door behind her, Jean went down the hall and down the stairs. On the ground floor she glanced out the foyer window and saw the dory nosing its way onto the beach. She flung open the door, running down the dune road. She halted at the top edge of the road and waved at the two figures now beside the bow of the dory, and as she scrambled down the dune she saw one wave back. That would be Ferris, of course, she knew. She ran across the sand to him and saw the old man, Enoch, watching her with bitter hostility in his eyes. Ferris stood silently, his face unsmiling, waiting, but she caught the hope in his eyes. Jean spoke quickly, wasting neither time nor words on amenities.

"I think Hobart Weatherby wants to do the right thing," she began. "I know I do. He's asked the government experts for a report on the problem here." She explained what had been decided and why, but when she'd finished she saw not understanding, not agreement, but fury in the old man's blazing eyes.

"Words, that's all," he shot out at her. "Words and lies. Just more of nothing."

"That's not so," Jean replied, her own anger flaring. "You'd all be better off with a proper, scientific report on what's happening. It'd tell everybody what should be done to meet the problem."

"There'll never be any report," Enoch said. "It's just another way to put us off again. Well, there'll be no more waiting by us, no more."

Enoch turned on Ferris, his anger spilling from him like sparks from a blowtorch. "I told you she'd not do anything," he said darkly. "She's no better than Weatherby. Their talk and our lives, the way it's always been, the way it always will be until we change it."

Jean wanted to deny the old man's bitter words, but he turned on her again, his parchment face a mask of fury. "You'll get from here if you know what's good for you," he said. "You'll get from here and stop backing old Weatherby."

"I'm not backing anybody," Jean cried out, but Enoch was swinging his spare frame into the dory.

"You go on," Ferris said to the man. "I'll be along soon." He shoved the prow of the dory free, and Enoch roared out with the wind carrying off his angry shouts at them. Jean saw the disappointment in Ferris's eyes.

"This won't help things," he said evenly. "I don't know that I can control the others much more. I'm afraid for you." His face grave, his eyes probed hers. "Anger has no mind," he said. "It explodes. It strikes out at the handiest victim."

"And that's me," Jean said. "But I'm trying to help. I thought the report was a good idea."

"It'll take months, probably," Ferris said. "Never heard of a government report that didn't."

"Months?" Jean frowned. "Oh, no, I don't think so. I just never thought about that part of it."

"Jock Sutherland's trawler was nearly struck by a tanker in the morning fog yesterday," Ferris said. "The best spot we've found offshore is right in the main channel out of Cabot Strait into the Atlantic."

"Please ask them to wait a little longer," Jean said. "I'll find out what I can about the report." Her hands pressed against the big man's chest as she looked up at him. "You do believe me, don't you, Ferris?" she asked.

"What I believe doesn't count," he said.

"It does to me," Jean said. His arms tightened around her, pulling her to him, his eyes were dark lights.

"You're a strange one, Jean Burroughs," he said. "You're too beautiful for your own good, I think. Maybe you should leave here before there's real trouble."

"No, I can't," Jean said instantly. "Not till I prove to your people that I wasn't lying, that I want to help."

Even as she said the words, she knew she was making up rational reasons for something that held no reason at all in it. She had to stay, just as she'd had to come, she realized in fright. "Hold me, Ferris," she whispered, suddenly trembling. His arms tightened around her, and his head reached down, and she felt his lips on hers, tasted the salt on them, and let the power of his embrace stop her trembling. Then, abruptly, he pulled away and started to leave, casting a last look back at her, his eyes deep with unspoken thoughts. Jean turned and headed back to the house, suddenly aware that the afternoon was at an end and the purple gray of night had started to creep across the sea.

The burning fury of the old man, Enoch, and Ferris's disappointed fears lay heavily on her, and she went into the house, angry and dissatisfied. She went to the phone, got Hobart Weatherby's number and dialed it. The lawyer's voice was surprise, first, then affable caution.

"How long will it take to get that report, Mr. Weatherby?" she asked directly.

"Oh, I can't say that, my dear," the man answered. "I haven't any idea how much information the bureau has already compiled on this matter."

"Can you give me some idea?" Jean persisted. "By next week? In ten days?"

"Oh, I hardly think that soon," Hobart Weatherby said smoothly.

"Longer than ten days?" Jean asked sharply. The man's voice remained calm. "Considerably longer, I'd guess. At least a month," he said. "Maybe two."

"I thought it'd be a matter of days," Jean said. "This puts a different light on the picture."

"Not at all, my dear," Hobart Weatherby said. "Just a little more time involved. Being right often takes a little time."

"Then I think that meanwhile the cove ought to be opened for fishing," Jean said.

"Why, if you want that, it's your right to do so," the lawyer said. "Why don't we have dinner at my place in a few days and talk it over again then. I don't like to see you make hasty decisions that could hurt the people you're trying to help."

"I don't want to do that, of course," Jean agreed. "All right, I'll be in touch with Bob about dinner."

She hung up and went to her room even more dissatisfied and angry with herself. Why didn't she just up and leave Hawk's End, she asked herself. She certainly wasn't finding the peace and quiet she had wanted. Or had she really sought that? Had Ferris been right that first day on the beach? Was she trying to punish herself, determined to come here and stay out of some masochistic urge? Guilt over Evan, she asked silently. It was more than enough. The powers of guilt were strong and complex. But what of the other powers, the ones Amantha called the powers of darkness? Damn, she swore silently. Why did the woman's ridiculous ramblings keep intruding on her thoughts? Why couldn't her own rational explanations satisfy her? Why, why, why? Questions without answers, too many of them. And the big, gaunt woman implied she knew answers. That was the core of it, Jean told herself, Amantha Colburn's implied wisdom that did the damage. Was it just that, the girl asked herself honestly, was it only *implied* wisdom? The woman had been right about the cornerpost. No animal had sent it crashing. And, her hands clenching tightly, Jean knew the gaunt woman had been uncomfortably close to the truth about being called here to Hawk's End. A tremendous wave of impatience seized the girl. She had to tear apart the woman's wild statements or she would have no peace of mind at all. Turning, she ran from the house, halting for a moment in the crispness of the dusk wind.

There was still a little light left to the day, and she hurried toward where the land rose in a rock-strewn hill. Glancing back, she saw the old house watching her, looking after her like some giant beetle certain of its victim's return. Why did she feel that way about the derelict old house, she questioned herself. Why didn't she just see it as a thing of splintered boards and sagging roofline? Why did it have its own malevolent presence for her? She couldn't blame that on Amantha's dire words. She had felt the house's malignant presence the first moment she had stood before it.

Hurrying upward, Jean saw the narrow footpath appear that Bob had spoken of, and she made her way up the winding passage. The rocks grew steeper on each side of her and broken and bent trees were misshapen sentinels. The grass, hard brush growth, fought for its place with the flat-sided rock, and the path rose more sharply. She had just turned a sharp bend when the house stood before her, a cabin amid the surrounding rocks, sitting there as if a giant hand had dropped it there. The roof was thatched, the sides stone and mortar, and a thin line of smoke curled from a crooked chimney. A huge cat, gray and black striped, stood in the doorway, and Jean could see through the open door into the room. She walked forward and called out. There was no answer, and she halted at the doorway. The cat moved into the room, looking up at her with yellow, baleful eyes. Jean saw a fireplace with a fire in it, a big black kettle over the flames. The cabin appeared to be one huge room. There was a half-drawn curtain across one end with a wooden bed behind it. A rough-hewn table stood in the center of the floor, and Jean called the woman's name again. There was still no reply, and she moved a few paces into the room, letting her eyes travel around the big room. From the wooden crosspieces of the roofline, hardly more than an arm's length up, she saw various amulets hanging, some of wood, some of silver, some of stone. She recognized opal, ruby, and garnet. Over the fireplace she saw the book Amantha had had at the house, leaning on a half-dozen others.

"What do you want here?"

The question, exploding the stillness, made the girl jump, and she whirled to see Amantha Colburn framed in the doorway, almost filling it, an orange cat in her arms.

"I came to see you," Jean said, finding her voice.

"I don't want you up here," the woman said.

"Afraid I'll contaminate your place?" Jean shot back, more bitterness than sarcasm in her voice.

"It's not your fault," the big woman said, moving into the room. "But I still don't want you here. Say your piece and get out."

"There are too many things around here unfinished, mostly the things you've said," Jean began. "And that red glow that moves on the water. I saw it again last night."

The woman nodded, and once again Jean saw a strange expression creep into Amantha Colburn's eyes, almost a look of pity.

"I think you know what it is," Jean said. "Why won't you tell me?"

The expression in the woman's eyes didn't change, and Jean felt her skin grow prickly. "You really believe it, don't you," the girl said. "You really believe I'm possessed."

"I know it," Amantha said in the same certain tone she had used about the cornerpost, the rock slide, and the strange red glow.

"Another soul, another spirit, you said," Jean went on. "Why me? Why did it wait for me?"

"It had to wait for the exact right moment in the exact right person," Amantha said. "It wouldn't have been possible otherwise. It takes an exact coming together of all the right elements for the possession of another person. I don't know what made you the one chosen, but it's happened."

"Who made it happen? Who waited for me?"

"Fiona MacFie," Amantha Colburn said. The picture of the strong-faced young woman in the shattered frame flashed in front of Jean.

"She lived in the old house," the girl said and the woman nodded. Feeling not at all ridiculous, Jean asked again.

"Who was she? Why would her spirit wait for me?"

The big woman sat down beside the table and gestured to Jean to sit in front of her.

"It was eighteen-hundred and ten and if you can imagine it, the house at Hawk's End sparkled and glistened," Amantha began. "There were servants and carriages and parties almost every night. Fiona MacFie was a wealthy young woman. She was proud, headstrong, and arrogant. Some said she had a streak of cruelty. She could ride, sail, and hunt, but most of all she loved to sail. Young, handsome men were no problem for Fiona MacFie, and she loved them all alike until there came here to New Scotland a young man named Aran Connare.

"He was a shipbuilder's apprentice and he fell in love with Fiona and, for the first time, she seemed to love, too. She let him announce their engagement and, later, their wedding day. Aran Connare spent all his spare time building a lovely boat for Fiona as a bridal present on which they were to sail on their honeymoon.

"But one day Aran Connare came to the house and found Fiona making love to someone else. It was said that, despite her love for Aran, she decided it was beneath her to marry a shipbuilder's apprentice. She refused to see Aran again and, in the way that was hers, she was heartless. Aran Connare cursed her, and on the night that was to have been their wedding night, he set his bridal boat afire with himself at the helm and sailed out from Rock Island with it ablaze. Fiona MacFie was giving a party that night, but she saw the bridal boat sailing past, aflame. They say she screamed for three days and was never the same again. She closed herself in the big house and saw no one except the servants.

"On certain nights from then on, the burning bridal boat sailed in front of the house, a light Fiona couldn't help seeing even through closed shutters. It's said she would come out on the widow's walk and call to Aran to come to her until the light went away. When she finally died years later, her spirit was still cursed by Aran Connare, doomed never to rest until it had satisfied Aran Connare's vengeance. To do that, it had to find someone to possess and destroy as she had destroyed Aran Connare's love.

"The light of Fiona MacFie's bridal boat is still seen sailing from Rock Island. You saw it yourself."

Amantha Colburn fell silent. Jean rose, turning to the door, her body bathed in cold perspiration. She began to walk, and the walk became a run as she flew out of the cabin, racing down the narrow footpath, stumbling against the rocks in the dark. Her mind a whirling, spinning thing, she ran until the great black bulk of the house loomed up in front of her and she raced inside, slamming the door behind her. In her room she latched the door and fell onto the bed, hearing the harsh sound of her breathing, feeling her clothes clinging to her as if she'd been thrown into the sea. Finally she got up and stripped, drying her body off and putting on a pair of lounging pajamas. Forcing herself to stop trembling, she lit a lamp and then put on the one in the hall, making herself do things as calmly as possible. But inside her room again, she latched the door and sank weakly down onto the bed, her hands again wet. No, she said firmly to herself, things like this just don't happen. She said it again aloud, hearing the sound of her voice in the silence of the old house, a hollow, mocking sound. She was being a child, she said to herself, being taken in by old stories, letting fancy run away with fact. She had to look at it calmly and sort imagination from reality. Stretching herself out on the top of the bed, she watched the wavering light of the lamp as she began to go over each thing in detail. Searching her mind with a silent desperation, she fought to hold onto reason and common sense logic, but the story of Fiona MacFie had its own logic and its own reason, and there was no denying it any longer. So much was suddenly clear now, with a terrifying clarity, beginning with that moonless night when she had sat up in bed and knew she had to come here to the house at Hawk's End. The legend of Fiona MacFie was but a strange parallel, she tried to tell herself and turned from her own shattered answer. There were too many things now that burned inside her, too many questions no reasoned explanation could satisfy. She went over every detail again and again as she lay in the flickering lamplight, and each time the answer was the same. She was as someone going through a hundred doors and always coming out at the same place. Fact hadn't separated from fancy, but had merged together to bring her a new, chilling reality. The unreal had become the real and she lay quiet, shocked and overwhelmed and frightened with a fright that was like no other she had ever known.

Even fleeing had been denied her, and she knew that now. She had to stay and wait and find the way to regain her own self, or, the girl shivered, die a prisoner. But whose prisoner, she asked herself. Who really possessed her? Was it Fiona MacFie or was it Evan? Or was it she who had sought punishment, had sought her possessor? Was Evan telling her things he could not make her hear when he was alive?

The thoughts kept racing through her mind, one more chilling than the other, and she had no idea how long she had lain there when she caught the short flash of light on the window. Getting up quickly, she saw the window pane wet with a fine rain and she peered into the blackness of the night. The brief instant of light flashed again, as though it were from a flashlight, and then it was gone. She waited at the window, trying to pierce the dark with her tired eyes, and finally she turned away. She was almost back to the bed when she heard the sound outside, a dull, thudding sound, as if someone had stumbled; then the heavy crash of the big door knocker boomed through the cavernous hallway. She took the lamp and went into the hallway where the other lamp still burned. The door sounded again, more insistently this time. Through the side window she could see the small drops of rain pebbling the glass. It was hardly the night nor the hour for callers. Drawing a deep breath, she put the lamp on the small holder alongside the door. The doorknob felt cold against her hand as she pulled the heavy door open and let the lamplight flicker over the tall figure standing there.

"Damn, this is a helluva place to get to," she heard the voice say, and then she heard her own voice, half a sob and half a cry of delight, and she was wrapped around the tall figure, her arms holding him tight. "Ted! Oh, God, Ted!" she cried out as she was carried back into the house. She let go and dropped down to the floor as the tall, sandy-haired man, unruly hair carelessly falling over his forehead, grinned down at her. "Now, that's the kind of welcome I like," he said.

Jean looked up at Ted Holbrook, hardly able to believe she wasn't dreaming. His hand cupped under her chin reassured her she wasn't. "You're in one piece yet, anyway," he said. "My car's back somewhere, in one of those blasted sand dunes. Took a corner too fast," he added sheepishly. "I'll get it pulled loose tomorrow."

"Then that light I saw, that was you?"

"My flashlight. It conked out on me after three minutes or so. But then anybody can have equipment that works. This adds a touch of the unexpected to things, makes everything an adventure."

His eyes were scanning the staircase, taking in the old wood of the hallway. "You wouldn't have anything to drink, would you?" he asked.

"No, I've been doing without and haven't missed it. But I'll make you some tea. Come on, let's go into the kitchen."

"Better than nothing. I've been driving all damn night," Ted Holbrook said, following her into the high-ceilinged old kitchen where two heavy logs glowed in the fireplace.

"Ted Holbrook, what in heaven are you doing here?" Jean asked as she poured water into an iron kettle and hung it over the logs.

"I got your damn letter, that's what I'm doing here," he said, and she turned to him, her eyes wide, remorse coloring them at once.

"Oh, Ted, I'm sorry. I didn't mean for it to upset you," she said. "I just wanted to write and tell you what had been happening." She wanted to stay cool and controlled but suddenly she felt her lower lip trembling, felt the rush of tears flooding into her eyes and then she was in his arms, her head pressed against his shoulder, hearing her deep sobs. It seemed so natural, and why shouldn't it, she realized. She'd been crying on that shoulder for the past months.

"Easy does it, Jeanie girl," she heard him say quietly and she pulled back, wiping her eyes dry with the back of her hand.

"I'm sorry, Ted," she murmured. "I didn't mean to do that. Force of habit, I guess."

"Suppose you sit down and tell me what's been going on here while I make the tea," he said, pressing her firmly into one of the deep-bottomed wood chairs. "Flesh out that letter for me, gorgeous."

It had always been easy to talk to Ted, and the words poured out of her. She left out nothing, and when she was finished she was drained and white. Ted's hazel eyes were coolly amused though a small frown hid beneath the lock of sandy hair that hung over his forehead. He had stretched his long, thin form out with his feet resting on one of the other chairs.

"That's got to be the weirdest story around," he said. "That's weird enough but it seems to me that you might be swallowing some of this. You aren't really, are you, Jeanie?"

Her eyes were round, grave as she looked up at him. "I didn't want to, Ted. I tried not to," she replied. "But there's no other answer anymore. Don't you see how it all fits, Ted? From my coming here to now, it all ties together. I'm scared, Ted, but I can't look away anymore."

"Of course there are other answers," Ted frowned, sitting up in the chair. "There are no forces or astral bodies or whatever the hell you want to call them going around possessing people."

"Ted, you know there are strange psychic things," Jean said quietly. "We used to talk about them."

"Hell, we used to talk about a lot of things," Ted said. "But not this kind of thing."

"Face facts, you used to say to me, Ted. Face facts. All right, face them. That cornerpost almost killed me. That's fact. It tore loose all by itself. That's fact, too. No animal smashed it loose, no wind blew, no logical, rational force made it fall."

"It could have given way on its own. The vibrations of this old morgue from the storm. One vibration too much and it gave way. That's the way those things happen, even with metal. They call it metal fatigue, there."

"And the rocks that almost killed me. That's fact, too. You really think an earth tremor struck just at that exact spot where I was sitting?"

"Stranger things have happened, Jeanie."

"And the burning glow on the water. I've seen it twice, now. It wasn't my imagination."

Ted frowned. "I haven't an answer for that one but I'm sure there is one," he said. "A good, sound, logical answer."

"Oh, Ted, don't you see there are too many things to write off as coincidences? I was called here, I know that now. Amantha Colburn was right about that, too. No one here knew what had happened with Evan; I'd never heard of Fiona MacFie. Yet I'm here, and there's too much in that to just write off."

"Look, Jeanie, your facts are facts, but you're interpreting them all wrong. You've run into an old legend that just happens to parallel an event in your own life and it's hit you hard."

He took her by the shoulders, and his eyes were hard under his frown as he looked at her. "Dammit, Jeanie, I just can't believe in spiritual forces possessing someone. At another time, another climate, you wouldn't go with it like you have, either."

"What do you mean another time?"

"You're vulnerable. You're still carrying Evan inside yourself. This fits in perfectly with your own guilt feelings."

"Or is it the other way around, Ted?"

"Come back to Boston with me," Ted said. "This is no place for you, certainly not now. Between the angry fishermen and that crazy, cackling woman you've got here you'll wind up a basket case."

"No, I can't go, Ted. That's part of it, too. I couldn't go if I wanted to. Something's holding me here."

"You're holding yourself here."

"Maybe," Jean reflected. "But even so, if I left now I'd feel like an unfinished book with a part of me missing, unexplained, unanswered. I'd be worse than when I came here."

Ted let a long sigh escape him as Jean leaned her head on his chest. "But you're wonderfully sweet to have come up," she said. "And it's really wonderful to have you here but I've got to go my own way on this thing. I've got to find out the final truth for myself, and I'm the only one who can find out."

"No matter where it leads?"

"No matter where."

"I'm not sure I buy that," Ted said. "But I'll sleep on it. I've a room in town, at a little place that had a sign saying they took in tourists. You can spend the day with me tomorrow, can't you?"

"Yes, of course," Jean answered quickly. "I had a tentative dinner date to confirm but that can wait."

"Charming the local talent already?" Ted grinned down at her. "The truth, girl."

"Maybe. A little, I guess. Bob Weatherby's very nice, easy to take. And there's Ferris Duncan."

"Ah, the fisherman you mentioned in your letter."

"Yes. He's very different from anyone I've ever known," Jean said. "There's a quiet, inner strength to him. Perhaps he's what I need."

She saw the cool amusement in Ted's eyes, an expression he usually wore. "I've an errand to do in the morning," Jean said. "If I'm not back when you come, just wait."

"Tomorrow, doll," he said, brushing her forehead with his lips. It was the way he'd always said goodnight to her and she watched him go off, the fine rain and the dark swallowing up his figure. She hurried back to bed for the few hours left till morning, feeling warmed by Ted's visit. But that was so like him, just as it was like him to try to calm her fears. And it was like him to turn away from that which went deeper than the surface realities. He could be concerned and wonderfully understanding. He could use wit and sharp perception to make truths reveal themselves. But the strength she needed to resist what had seized her, the strength to find out where reality lay, that she would have to draw from herself, or elsewhere.

She closed her eyes, drained and exhausted, knowing she had to go forward on the course she had quietly set for herself—or that had been set for her. If there were other answers, she would have to find them herself.

CHAPTER FIVE

She woke late and heard Amantha in the kitchen. The morning appeared cool and the sun fought its way through a thin layer of clouds. She dressed quickly, putting on her jeans and a bright orange and white print blouse and a cardigan over it. In the hall she exchanged silent glances with Amantha and then hurried outside, feeling the woman's eyes following her.

Looking across the edge of the land, she could see the dim bulk of Rock Island in the distance and her lips tightened. The island had intrigued her ever since Ferris had told her no one would set foot on it. Of course, now she understood why. Fear, superstition, a kind of folk wisdom, or as Ferris had said, the plain unwillingness to tempt fate. But now it was more than intriguing. Now it was a challenge, a place she had to visit and it pulled on her as she had been pulled here to the house at Hawk's End. What did she think to find there, she asked herself. Perhaps the final confirmation of all, perhaps a hope to cling to, perhaps nothing, and that might of itself be something.

She had turned to go to her car when she saw Bob Weatherby driving down the dune road toward her, waving an arm from the window.

"Morning," he called cheerily as he pulled to a halt. "Had to come up this way and decided to stop by and say hello. Met a friend of yours getting his car pulled back onto the road."

"Yes, he came unexpectedly last night," Jean said. "Ted Holbrook's an old and very good friend."

"How good a friend?" Bob smiled.

"Not that good, if I read you right," Jean replied. "But he's a real friend. He's helped me a lot. I promised to spend the day with him so we'll have to put off dinner with your father."

"Another day or so won't make any difference to anyone," Bob said, and Jean held her frown back. Every day made a difference to Ferris and Enoch, she knew. Their attitude was very different than the easy, calm approach that Bob and his father brought. "Going back to town?" she asked. "You can drop me off at that place you said rented boats. I've decided to get a little boat and moor it in the cove. I saw a small dock sticking out from the near end there."

"Yes, it's been there for a hundred years and it's still in good shape," Bob replied. "Get in, I'll take you to Hank Thompson's."

Bob turned the car around and they went back along the dune road, slowing as they reached the tow truck and the small foreign car, a dark green MG, now back on the road. Ted stood by it as the truck driver took off the towing chains. As Bob slowed, Ted leaned down to wave at them. His grin was lazy; his eyes cool, appraising. Jean smiled to herself. There was little that Ted ever missed. He had a photographer's eye and a mind that clicked with the speed of a shutter.

The boatyard turned out to be a collection of small dinghies, dories, and one old sloop. Hank Thompson, a dour-faced man, accepted her check for the rental on Bob's word and she selected a sturdy, weathered dory with a thirty-five horsepower outboard on it. She added an extra drum of gasoline, which she had stored in the bow plus a small mooring buoy.

"I'll sail to the cove and tie up," she called to Bob as she stepped into the boat.

"I'll meet you there," he called back. "Be careful. These waters are no lake. I hope you can handle a boat."

"Handled one every year at the Cape for ten years," she said, pulling on the starter. The motor coughed once, then came smoothly to life, and the boatman cast off the bowline.

She headed from the small harbor, past the houses of the town that crowded the edge, the fishing trawlers tied up by the wharves, and then she was into the open sea and the wind slapped at her at once. The boat rode the long swells with ease, and she turned north up the shoreline. Her eyes peered across at the low outline of Rock Island in the distance. It would have to wait till tomorrow, after she'd finished her day with Ted. If she knew Ted, a hundred and one things would be demanding he return by tomorrow. She turned her gaze from the island and increased speed, hugging the shoreline. As she passed the beach and saw the gray bulk of the old house, the line of rocks extending down from it to the water, she headed out further to round the point of the cove. The fishing trawler appeared just as she reached the point, coming south, passing her on the starboard side less than a dozen or so feet away. She saw the tall, spare figure of the old man, Enoch, standing at the rail, and his eyes blazed at her. And across the water the hate of the man reached out to her. The trawler, a thirty-five footer she estimated, passed on, and she rose on its wake and then turned into the cove. The small dock beckoned, and slowing the boat, she nosed up to it and tossed a line over the corner piling. She was securely moored in moments and she hurriedly began to clamber up the steep side of the land, waving at Bob, who waited at the top for her.

He reached a hand down and pulled her up the last few feet. "You'll come sailing with me some afternoon?" Jean asked, and Bob nodded happily.

"Don't take any chances in these waters," Bob said. "Weather changes fast up here."

"I'll be careful," Jean said as they walked back to the house and Bob drove off, his last glance at her a narrowed, studying one. She saw the small, dark green MG parked off to the side and she hurried into the house. Ted's long form was spread out in one of the chairs in the library. He flashed a smile at her as she entered. "Been waiting long?" she asked. "I'm sorry I'm late. I'll only be a minute changing."

"Take your time," Ted said. "It's been an educational wait. I exchanged three or four words with your housekeeper. Real personality kid, that woman. And you had a visitor."

"A visitor?" Jean echoed, frowning.

"Mount Rushmore," Ted said blandly, and the girl's frown deepened.

"Stone-face ... your fisherman, Ferris Duncan."

"Ted Holbrook! What a terrible thing to say," Jean exclaimed and saw Ted's slow grin. "Whoever said I was nice?" he retorted. "He'd heard about your renting a boat and he wanted to talk to you about it."

"Did he say why?"

"Are you kidding?" Ted tossed back. "Conversation around here is something of six or seven words. He said he'd get back to you. But I'm curious myself. Just what prompted you to rent a boat all of a sudden?"

"It's not all of a sudden," Jean lied smoothly. "You know I like to sail around. You know I've done it every summer at the Cape."

"Yes, but I know you, Jeanie Burroughs. Are you planning something on your own?" he queried, his eyes narrowed, watching her as a cat watches a mouse.

"Just sailing around a bit," Jean replied, silently congratulating herself on a good answer. Ted grunted, his eloquent grunt reflecting acceptance more than belief, but he gave her a small smile. "Get changed," he said. "Let's have some fun."

She turned and hurried to her room, putting on the blue low-cut dress there'd be little chance or time to wear up here with anyone else. When she returned to the library, Ted's cool appraisal couldn't hide his appreciation.

"You've got to go back to Boston with me," he said. "You are definitely in the wrong place."

"Don't be too sure," she answered. "All this window dressing isn't really that important."

"It sure is to me, girl," he said and hurried her to the car. They drove aimlessly, following roads neither of them knew, finding small places of harsh beauty, a pond with snow geese resting and tall cattails, a spot of purple heather on a hillside, old fences and a waterwheel, and the day drifted into evening. They had driven nearly a hundred miles down the coast; they found a good restaurant that was relaxed, almost sophisticated, and they ate leisurely. Ted had her laughing long and hard as he described the electronic difficulties of the last John Cage concert he attended, and when the day finally ended and they returned to the old house it was past midnight. She leaned against Ted's tall figure.

"Thanks for everything, Ted," she said softly. "For coming, for being concerned, for your letters."

"I was concerned before you left, if you remember?" he said and she smiled to herself. He had never agreed that she should go off by herself. "It's been good leaning on you again," she said.

"Watch it, girl," Ted said and she looked up into his coolly contained gaze. "It could be habit-forming."

"I'll watch it," she promised. "Stop by in the morning?" she added. She almost said, *before you go,* but decided against it.

"Definitely," he said, kissing her lightly on the forehead. Jean latched the big door and undressed quickly. In bed she clutched the evening to her, knowing it had been an oasis of fun, a moment snatched from whatever lay before her. As a gust of wind blew against the old house and she heard the creak and groan of it, the chill feeling of being held, being trapped, came over her. She looked across the room to the window and the blackness of the night outside. There was no glow from the sea this night and she turned on her side and slept.

Morning came dressed in a gray mist so thick it seemed to rain without raining, giving everything a shiny, wet patina that made even an old rotted piece of wood seem fresh. Jean put on a light but warm weather jacket and heavy dungarees and hurried outside to scan the water, her lips tight in angry disappointment. It was still morning and the fog that blanketed the sea and the land had lots of time to blow away. But there was no wind, and the sound of the unseen surf was ghostly in the stillness. Amantha's huge figure materialized out of the grayness, and Jean saw the housekeeper go into the opened front door, pausing to look around until she saw where Jean stood near the edge of the rocks. The fog, gray and unmoving, shrouded the land and covered the rocks and grass with wetness. Wind, Jean whispered to herself. Wind could blow it all away in an hour, perhaps less. But she knew these days, had seen many of them at the Cape, and the shroud of gray stayed on for as long as it could, unwilling to tear itself apart. These were the days when nothing moved on shore or sea, not birds, not ships, not men.

Out there, in the grayness, Rock Island lay, and she felt it mocking her. Scanning the few feet she could see around her, she swore impatiently and started back to the house. The four o'clock wind was her only hope for this day, she knew. Or perhaps a noon sun hot enough to burn away the fog. She was at the door when she heard the sound of a motor, the low, deep throb of the MG, and she watched the little car materialize out of the fog and Ted's long form unfold from it.

"Made it," he said. "And I was going to shoot some pictures today."

Jean felt her frown appear. "I thought you'd be starting back this morning," she said. His eyebrows raised and his eyes danced at her. "Oh, didn't I tell you? I decided to stick around a bit longer," he said. "How about some coffee?" he said, starting to brush past her. She caught his arm and looked at him, her face unsmiling.

"Hold it, Ted, old friend," she said. "I know what you're doing and why, and I can't let you do it. You've probably ten assignments waiting unfinished and you're not going to neglect your work because of me. Besides, whatever is here, whether I'm right or you are, it's something I've got to fight out myself."

"Maybe I'm more concerned about other mistakes you might make, about you and Mount Rushmore."

"I wish you'd stop calling Ferris that just because he's quiet."

"I know, the strong, silent type is always appealing. They give the impression of being deep thinkers."

"That's often so."

"Only once in a while. Mostly they're silent because they just haven't anything to say."

"Ted Holbrook, if I didn't know better I'd think you were jealous."

"You know better so forget it. But you're a romanticist, Jeanie, and in your upset mood you can't think straight about anything."

"Is that so?" Jean flared. Ted smiled affably. He could be infuriatingly assured, Jean thought.

"He's not for you, Jeanie girl," Ted said blandly.

"Now you're an expert on who's for me?" she bit out. His smile never changed. "No, just who's not," he said.

Jean glared at him, watching him cheerfully ignore her. "I'll be in town on the phone for most of the day," he said. "I've got to tell Harper Cannon what to do with the stuff I left for him, and you know Harper, he'll be calling me back every fifteen minutes with questions. I'll have to sit by the phone." Ted ducked low to peer up at the sky out of the window and then tossed Jean a genial grin as she stood tight-lipped, watching him.

"There'll be no sailing around in this muck," he commented cheerfully. "So you can't get into trouble that way. I'll be in touch later."

Jean watched him leave, glowering after him from the door. The fog remained thick, and she spent the rest of the morning pacing back and forth impatiently. Noon saw the fog unchanged, but at three o'clock she went to the cove, making her way down the slope to the little dock. She felt a coolness against her face. There was a wind, slight, but still a wind, and the gray blanket had lifted a few feet. She scanned the water, frowning in thought. The fog could be strictly shoreline, hugging the warmer temperature of the land. She had seen that before where, a mile out to sea, the winds had blown the fog away. It was a chance she'd take, particularly with Ted busy and out of the way. The unseen island called to her, insistent, demanding. Besides, the fog had lifted just enough for her to see to navigate and, if the fogbank extended out beyond a mile, she'd just turn around and head back. She pulled the starter, and the outboard came alive at once. Holding the motor to a low purr, she headed from the cove and was on the quiet, glassy water of the open sea in a few minutes. Under the fog she glimpsed the sand of the beach, and she turned the boat east for Rock Island, still invisible behind the barrier of gray ahead. She peered back and took her bearings again under the layer of fog that remained lifted enough for her to see. The beach was directly astern, and the point of her cove to the north. Turning, she concentrated on sailing the dory in a straight line toward where the fog still hugged the sea. As she neared the heavy fogbank, she heard the clanging of a buoy, and she scanned the sea to find it. The calm waters let it clang only intermittently, but finally she saw it, a hundred yards to her right, a big, red buoy with its pyramidlike framework encasing the bell. It was obviously a channel marker for deep-draught boats. Heading directly on, the fog rose up in front of her and she slowed the boat, looking for a break in the grayness. But there was none, the fogbank a thick, blanketing curtain. Dare she risk it, she asked herself grimacing. It could run for only a hundred feet, and then she'd be through it in clear water. Or, it could run for miles and she'd be hopelessly lost. Damn, she said silently. The afternoon wind hadn't come up, not enough, anyway, and it would be dark in little more than an hour. She couldn't risk it, not in these waters, and then, as if to help her make up her mind, she saw that the fog was closing down quickly, squeezing together the narrow layer of clear air behind her.

Lips pressed tightly together in angry frustration, she swung the dory around in a tight circle. As she did so the motor coughed, gagged, then quit. Frowning, Jean yanked at the starter again. The motor caught, held for an instant, and then died. The girl glanced up at the fog and saw it had come down nearly a foot in but a few minutes. She knew that the narrow layer of visibility between her and the distant shoreline would be gone in another few minutes, and she pulled frantically on the starter again. It caught, but once more the motor coughed and died.

"Damn, it's not the starter!" she yelled aloud. She flipped up the lid on the gas tank and peered down the gasline, seeking some obstruction perhaps. The girl's brow furrowed at once. It had been a full tank and she'd used hardly any, but there was no trace of gasoline visible. If there was a leak in the tank it didn't leak fast enough to prevent her from sailing from the boatyard to the cove. Casting another alarmed glance at the settling fog, she reached into the bow of the dory and seized the extra tin of gasoline she'd bought. She almost fell backwards as it came up in her hand light and empty. Gasping, she tore open the top and peered into the tin. It was completely empty, and she felt a coldness envelope her that was not the damp chill of the fog as it settled down to shroud the little boat. The tin had been emptied, siphoned off during the night, as had the gas tank. But cleverly, enough gas had been left for her to sail far enough from land, where the main currents would sweep her out to sea, and where she'd be too far to signal for help. The fog had settled upon her now, and she sat surrounded by grayness that was fast turning darker. Though the sea was calm she could feel the strength of the current pushing her farther out into the Atlantic. And now she was hopelessly lost in the swirling grayness, unable to determine which way to try to turn the boat with her hands. She dipped both hands into the water, recoiling for an instant from the coldness of it, and then paddled with both hands, turning the dory to the starboard. It was as good a guess as any, and she was about to attempt to move the boat forward, using her hands as paddles, when she heard the sound of the motor, low and soft in the fog. It seemed to be coming from off the starboard bow, but the thick fog played with the sound, first blanketing it, then letting it come through, then muffling it again. But the sound was coming nearer, and she sat up straight in the bow, trying to peer through the thickness of the fog. It could pass within a few yards of her and not see her, she realized. "Here!" she called out. "Over here! Disabled craft over here!"

She counted off fifteen seconds between each call, timing her calls like that of a foghorn's steady, intermittent blasts, and her voice sounded clear and loud in the gray silence. The motor grew louder, coming nearer and then, through the swirling haze, she saw the other boat, a dory, moving toward her, shrouded in trailing scarves of fog. Dimly, she saw a figure standing or on one knee at the stern, cloaked in a long oilskin slicker with a wide-brimmed "souwester" on.

She called out and waved. He could see her now as she saw him and the dory changed course slightly to come up on her along the port side. She watched the other boat swinging up to come alongside, moving ghostlike in the fog, and she heard the other boat's motor shut off. The tall figure picked up a long oar, starting to extend it, and Jean leaned forward to grasp the end of it. "Am I glad to see you!" she said as the other boat came abreast of her. She saw the oar rise and then, as her mouth opened in a gasp of shock, she saw the oar come down in a short, vicious arc. She managed to get her arm up as it smashed against her shoulder with shattering pain and she felt herself go sprawling on the bottom of the boat. Purple and yellow lights flashed in her head, and she struggled upright, shaking her head just enough to clear it as the oar came down again. Twisting her body, she half-fell across the center seat as the oar smashed down where she had been. She scrambled to the stern and saw the figure using the oar to paddle backward, coming alongside her again, and once more the figure swung the heavy oar and she felt it whistle over her head as she slumped to the bottom of the dory.

The tall figure was trying to kill her, and there was nothing ghostly in the way the oar slammed down onto the boat. Death was stalking her in the fog, vicious, sudden, and very real. And she had called out to it, she realized with grim irony. Whoever it was wanted to be sure she was dead, unwilling to trust the fog and the sea currents. She saw the boat as it drifted a few feet away and watched as the tall figure reached down into the stern. The sound of the motor coming on vibrated through the grayness, and the tall figure steered the boat alongside again. This time, holding the oar like a baseball bat, he swung it sideways, and Jean felt the splinters of wood as it crashed into the gunwale where she cowered. He swung the oar in the air again, and this time she watched him, forcing herself to stay still, waiting until the oar came down. As it descended she flung herself to one side and saw the sharp edge of it crash onto the top edge of the dory. She twisted back, throwing herself on top of it and feeling it tear from her assailant's grip. It skittered out over the side and she clutched for it, getting one hand on it before it slipped from her and splashed into the sea. Whirling, she saw that the boat had gone on a few feet and was circling to come back again. The tall figure, head bent low, fog shrouded, was more than a ghostly attacker, and now she saw the boat coming at her again, on the port side. She saw the figure reach down into the stern of the dory as the boat passed too far off and then disappeared for a moment in the fog. Jean felt her choking sob as, for a moment, she wondered if it had gone away to disappear as it had come. But she heard the sound of the motor returning, and she knew that death didn't give up so easily. Watching, hardly daring to breathe, she saw the boat appear again, heading toward her, moving fast now. The figure knelt at the stern, one arm upraised, holding something, and as the boat came by she saw him fling his arm forward and then the object was hurtling at her, long, ugly, pointed; in horror she saw the harpoon smash with tremendous force into the stern as she twisted aside. It pierced the weathered wood with ease, and she saw the sea come bubbling into the boat through the hole.

The craft had turned and was coming past again, closer this time, and the tall figure flung another harpoon, at closer range in a shorter, more downward arc. It whistled past her legs and slammed through the floorboards as she rolled across the bottom of the boat. Again she saw the old wood splinter as a huge gouge tore away, and this time the sea rushed in with force. She looked up, but the other boat was going on, vanishing into the fog, and she heard the sound of the motor fading away. The sea was clutching at her ankles already, and the dory was filling fast. The killer had decided to let the sea do his work after all. It had almost claimed the dory as it rose quickly to the edge of the gunwales. Jean threw off her shoes and swam from the boat, seeing it go down behind her. How long would the sea take to claim her, she wondered. Not long, she knew. Even though it wasn't winter yet, when a man lasted less than a minute in these icy waters, the cold seeped into her almost at once. She could feel it numbing her skin. Soon it would reach deeper into her, numbing her muscles next, robbing them of strength, and the rest would follow quickly. She swam, using long, powerful strokes, knowing that every bit of body heat she could generate delayed the end that much longer. But she also knew it was a losing contest, and she could be swimming farther into the sea. The blackness was all around her, and she could feel her legs stiffening from the cold and her teeth were beginning to chatter.

Then, as she tried to swim faster, she heard it, the soft, clanging sound. She turned on her back and floated, listening. The fog played tricks with sound, but she listened carefully, counting the intervals between each clang as she drifted. The sound was holding steady. She was drifting toward it, and she turned over and began to swim, pausing to tread water and listen every few moments. The bell was sounding louder now, and she renewed her efforts, but the cold had seized her in its inexorable grip. Her strength was failing, and each movement of her arms was a painful, slow thing. But the buoy sounded clearly now, just ahead somewhere, and then she saw it emerge from the fog. Fighting off the congealing cold, she lifted her arms again, forcing herself to go the short distance that seemed so long, and then she was beside it, getting a hand on its bottom crosspiece. She hung there for a long moment and then, with the cold sea reluctant to let go, she pulled herself up onto the broad base of the buoy. She felt it tip with her weight, the bell clanging loudly, and then right itself as she clung to it, wrapping her arms and legs around the triangular, steel frame. The air was dank and clammy and cold but without the numbing, deadly cold of the sea, and she let her breath return as the bell tolled with rythmic regularity.

Grateful for the calmness of the sea, she clung to the frame of the buoy, carefully shifting position whenever her arms grew stiff. So long as the fog stayed, the sea would remain calm, and by now Ted, at least, and perhaps others, would be searching for her. She knew Ted's logical mind. He'd check the dory and find it gone. But they could search aimlessly in the fog, she realized, looking out at the blackness, feeling the fog trail past her face, gently cruel in its mocking touch. She fought off fatigue and cold as she clung to the buoy, finding different ways to wedge herself into the steel framework with each change of position. The killer had gone, secure in the belief that it would be seen as just one more tragedy at sea, the result of her own stupidity. And, as she gazed at the night fog, she knew he might yet be right. Her arms hurt, and her one arm where the oar had hit it, was swollen. If the wind came up fast to blow the fog away and the sea grew rough, she could never hold to her precarious perch. She knew she hadn't the strength left. She moved her head from side to side, fighting the overpowering desire to sleep. She had just shifted position again when she heard the sound of the motor, and her eyes peered through the blackness. The sound came closer, and she felt her lips part to call, then close again. Was it help? Or was it death returning, probing the fog to be certain. She wanted to cry out but the memory of how close death had come seared her throat closed. The motor was near now, its sound throbbing through the fog. Her lips parted again, and a cry forced its way through her throat, and then she heard the voice, echoing through a megaphone.

"*AHOY OUT THERE!*" the voice cried. "Miss Burroughs. Coast Guard Patrol. If you can hear us, please answer. Miss Burroughs."

"Here!" Jean shouted, hearing the sob in her voice. "At the buoy, over here. Do you hear me?"

Her answer was the sharp sound of the motor increasing speed and the fog gave birth to the shape of a boat, gray white, moving slowly toward her, and then it was alongside her and hands were reaching for her, pulling her from the buoy.

It was later, when she was wrapped in warm blankets and the small patrol boat nosed its way through the fog, that she had a chance to question the young Coast Guard officer.

"A Mr. Ted Holbrook called us," he said. "He told us there was a good chance you'd headed out to Rock Island, and he gave us your point of departure. We set up a cross search pattern. We hoped you had reached Rock Island and were safe but fogbound on it."

"No, I never reached it, as you saw," Jean said. I never reached it because someone tried to kill me, she almost said, but she held her tongue. There was no one to accuse, no evidence to point to, nothing but her own words. It would sound like a wild tale she'd made up to explain her foolishness and the loss of the boat. She lapsed into silence and sat quietly as the patrol boat finally nosed into the small harbor of town. She saw the pier materialize in the fog, and the patrol boat was brought alongside. She freed herself of the warm blankets and climbed onto the pier. The fog was lighter here, wispier, and at the far end of the pier she saw the low silhouette of the waiting MG. A figure moved from the rail of the pier as she started up it, and she saw Ferris, his face grave, reaching out to hold her arm. "What happened, Jean?" he said.

He read the fear in her eyes, she knew, and without a word from her, knew it had been more than just getting lost in the fog. "Can you meet me on the beach tomorrow?" she said. "I'll tell you then."

He nodded. "After I get back," he said. "In the afternoon." He stepped aside and the Coast Guard officer came up to lead her to the car. Ted leaned over to open the door and she slid in, seeing the controlled fury in his eyes. He put the car in motion without a word, heading up the road from town.

"Thanks," she said finally. "I understand it was you who got the patrol boat out searching for me."

"Don't mention it," he bit out. "I'm out for Eagle Scout. This'll help a lot."

"You told them I'd headed for the island."

"It figured. Besides, I called your friend Weatherby and you weren't there. He's waiting to hear from me. I'll call him later."

"Thank you," Jean said quietly. "You think it was stupid, of course. You can't understand why I had to go."

"I understand you've used up your luck for the next ten years. I understand you're full of cockeyed ideas. Just where did they find you? That was a piece of sheer luck by itself."

"On the channel buoy," she said as he swung the car to a halt in front of the house.

"Where?" he frowned at her, and then she was against him, sobbing out everything that had happened, seeing the crashing oar and the hurtling harpoons again with vivid reality. She finished finally, and Ted let her sit still, pressed against his shoulder, till she stopped shaking. When they went into the house, he lighted the hall lamps and one in the library.

"Well, that settles it," he said. "Get your things. You're going back with me. Now, tonight."

"No, Ted," Jean said, surprised at the adamancy of her own voice.

"NO?" Ted exploded. "What do you mean, no? Somebody tried to kill you. You're not Miss Popularity here."

"But it didn't come off, and I think that's the end of it."

"You think that's the end of it. You sound as though you know who did it?"

"No, I couldn't see his face. I don't know. I just think it had to be someone from the town, one of the fishermen. And if it wasn't, then it had to be something else."

"Oh, God, Jeanie, not that possessed bit again. From what you told me this was real, damn real."

"Yes, it was real. But so was the cornerpost and so were the rocks, Ted," she said. She stepped closer to his long form. "Don't you see, Ted, I've come here to find myself," she said. "If I run from this, from anything here, I'll be running forever. I know that, Ted. I know it inside me. I'm sorry you can't understand that, and I don't blame you, but it's me and I can't feel any different."

"I sure as hell don't understand it," Ted said angrily. "But it's pure madness and I'm not having any part of it."

"I don't blame you, Ted. But thanks again, for tonight, especially. Now I'm going to bed, Ted. I'm tired, very tired."

He stalked from the house after casting her a last incredulous glance, and she went to her room. Despite her exhaustion, she drew a warm bath and let the water wash the sea from her and soothe her aching body. But in bed she couldn't wash away the closeness of death. How many more times would she escape its grip? Anyone could have done it this time. It was one of the fishermen, of course, one of those who didn't want her to exist any longer, one whose simple mind let him think that would end all his troubles. She saw the old man, Enoch, as he passed on the trawler yesterday. It could well have been him. It would have been simple enough to go to the cove in the night and siphon off the gasoline, then lie in wait for her to leave. And she had played her part perfectly, acting foolishly, driven by her own obsessions. If it had dawned clear and bright, the plan would have been changed, but only slightly. She would have sailed out a little further, and then, nearing the island, her little craft would have been helpless and a strong wind, usual that far out, would have swept her to sea. Perhaps, in its own way, the fog had been a blessing.

She saw Ted's angry eyes in front of her as she'd told him she couldn't run. Poor Ted. She didn't blame him. This wasn't for him. No words to the rescue here, no cleverness, no turning it all aside with the right phrase or the right drink. This was uncompromising reality, frightening, vivid, harsh. But perhaps, now that the attempt to kill her had failed, it was over. Perhaps. It was a good thought, but she fell asleep still feeling trapped, a victim of forces beyond her control, destined to wait for whatever the future held. During the night she tossed and turned and saw Evan Reed's face in her dreams, laughing at her, crying for her, and the night was long until finally she managed to sleep soundly as dawn touched the roof of the house at Hawk's End.

CHAPTER SIX

Jean woke with the ice of the sea still in her bones and the taste of death still in her mouth. She had slept late and, dressing in a nubby gray sweater and maroon slacks, she went into the kitchen. Amantha set a cup of tea in front of her, fastening the girl with a long stare.

"I heard," the woman said.

"How?" Jean asked sharply, feeling herself grow tense at once.

"Young Weatherby phoned. He said he'd be up later," the woman remarked, and Jean felt her body relax. Ted had promised to call Bob and had obviously done so.

"Someone deliberately tried to kill me," Jean said. "Nothing mysterious, nothing inexplicable, no being possessed about it." She watched Amantha intently and saw the woman's eyes meet hers.

"Wasn't there?" Amantha said, a statement, not a question.

"What do you mean?" Jean asked.

"The vengeance of Fiona MacFie's spirit brought you here to be destroyed," the woman said. "How it happens isn't important."

Amantha walked from the kitchen, and Jean sat very still in the chair, looking into the teacup, finally drinking the tea in one long pull. She went back to her room and counted the money in her checkbook. It would probably just cover the cost of the dory, and she made a mental note to go to the boatyard and settle up with Mr. Thompson.

When Bob arrived she was sitting at the edge of the ledge just above the rocks, looking out at the water now free of fog and sparkling brilliantly in the sun. He was kneeling beside her at once, holding her by the shoulders.

"You poor kid," he murmured. "The bastards. The stinking, stupid bastards. I'll find out who it was, Jean. It may take awhile, but I'll find out."

"It's over and done," Jean smiled. "I'm all right."

"No, whoever it was might try again. Why don't you leave here, Jean, for a while, anyway. Father and I'll handle things as we always have. When the report comes in we'll get in touch with you. I wouldn't give in to them until then, at least. Not after this."

"It doesn't seem right, does it?" Jean said uncertainly. "I don't know what's right to do."

"Dad's still waiting for you to come to dinner and talk about it again," Bob said. "Let's make it in a few days."

Jean nodded and felt his arms around her. "You keep me informed of what you're doing and where you're going," Bob said. "For a little while, at least. I'd feel better about it if you insist on staying here."

His eyes were darkened with concern, and his kiss on her cheek was tender. When he left she returned to her room and stretched out on the bed, realizing how tired and aching her body still was. Death had stalked her here at Hawk's End, death that came from yesterday and death that came from today. But there were friends here, too. There was also concern and perhaps love here, and maybe the balance would be enough. She drifted off to sleep as she lay atop the bed, her body demanding rest. When she woke it was late afternoon, and she jumped from the bed and raced to the window. Looking down at the beach she saw the figure waiting there, and she ran from the house to race along the dune road.

Ferris met her as she half-ran, half-fell down the nearest dune, his powerful arms holding her easily, his face grave, his deep eyes searching hers. As she stayed there in the strength of his arms he spoke to her. "Your friend from the city was down at the pier when we sailed this morning," he said.

"Ted?" Jean exclaimed. "What in heaven was he doing up at that hour, to say nothing of being down at the pier?"

Ferris shrugged. "He told me about last night," the big man said. "It wasn't one of us, Jean."

Jean gazed into his eyes and saw pain and truth in them. "You think it was Enoch, don't you?" he asked her, and she knew he saw the answer in her eyes.

"It wasn't," Ferris said. "He hates you, but he wouldn't do that."

"You can't be sure, Ferris," she said softly and saw him look out at the sea, wrestling with his own thoughts. When he looked back at her, there was more conviction than defensive pain in his eyes.

"No, I can't believe that," he said. "Not one of us. It couldn't have been." He pulled her to him suddenly, roughly, holding her like a rag doll in his arms, his deep eyes boring into her. "It's strange things that happen to you, Jean Burroughs," he said. "Strange things indeed."

"What do you think of old legends, Ferris?" she said into his chest. "Do the dead speak to us in their own ways?"

"I think nothing really dies," he said. "Things go on, in different shapes, in different ways. Some day maybe we'll know more." He held her to him, and she knew he would say no more. She stayed in his arms until he stepped back.

"Not one of us, it wasn't," he said again, and then he was gone, walking quickly with long, powerful strides. Jean walked back along the beach to the rocks and then, clambering onto them, climbed their irregular stairway to the top. It was the first time she'd been on them since the slide, and it gave her a sense of defiance as she looked back at them from the top. Going into the house, she looked back at the sea and the dim, dark bulk of Rock Island, framed against the night sky starting to touch the horizon. She could feel it beckoning to her, mockingly, and she turned away angrily, blaming her imagination for working overtime.

Amantha, with her coat draped over her shoulders, was just leaving, and the woman paused at the door, her deep-lined face seemed set in marble. The woman's brown-flecked, green eyes burned at Jean. *I am right,* they seemed to say. *You are possessed, Jean Burroughs, you are possessed. I know, I know.* The woman turned abruptly and hurried out, and Jean went into the kitchen. She wasn't hungry, and she nibbled on a roast beef sandwich with hot tea. Finishing quickly, she lighted a lamp and went into the library, stretching out on the old leather sofa there.

The night had closed down on the land. Only Ted hadn't stopped by. He'd probably left in anger and disgust, and perhaps in some fear. As she lay on the sofa, letting her thoughts flow freely, she half-smiled as she thought of how certain Ferris had been. Loyalty had made him refuse to accept the truth. It had to have been one of his people, probably the old man, Enoch. He was more than strong enough to have smashed the oar down on her and flung those harpoons with shattering force. Or it could have been any of those who'd been aboard the trawler as she'd passed it. Stubborn, thick people, Hobart Weatherby had characterized them. People like that were always certain of their convictions, possessed by them. She smiled ironically, and then a frown replaced the smile as she thought of Amantha. Certainly the big woman had an unyielding certainty of her own. Her absolute belief in the forces of the occult world was unshakable and buttressed by everyday applications she could argue with considerable logic. Perhaps Amantha was the possessed one, but was she possessed enough by them to insist they come true? Did she have to prove her prophecies to herself?

It wasn't impossible, Jean mused. The figure in the other boat could well have been Amantha. She was tall enough and powerful enough. But, Jean reminded herself, Amantha hadn't made the cornerpost fall nor the rockslide thunder down on her. Nor had she written the strangely parallel stories of Fiona MacFie and Jean Burroughs. Questions, more questions, the girl told herself. They kept spinning like a soundless carrousel that never slowed long enough to seize the brass rings which were the answers. She wrapped her arms tightly across her chest and thought of the strength that was in Ferris's embrace. She was still thinking of Ferris when she heard the sound of a car approaching and she rose to go to the door as the low silhouette of the MG drew to a halt.

"I thought you'd gone back to Boston," Jean said with honest surprise as Ted sauntered in, his hazel eyes looking down at her with cool appraisal.

"Not yet," he said. "I wanted to give you another chance."

"Let's not start that again, Ted," Jean said. "I told you yesterday...."

"I know, if you run you'll be running all your life," he interrupted. "All right, I'm here because I've decided I like it here. It's a nice, cozy, friendly spot."

He tossed a grin over her skeptical glance. "I've been conversing with the natives," he said blandly.

"So I hear," she replied stiffly.

"Had a visit from Mount Rushmore, did you?" he grinned. "Haven't changed my mind on that. Careful does it, Jeanie girl."

His bland assurance was infuriating, and she felt her lips tighten. "There's nothing wrong with Ferris Duncan. Please stop making it sound that way," she threw at him.

"Didn't say there was," he said. "But you must try him out on Mozart sometime," he added, his eyes cool circles of mocking amusement. "He'll probably think *Don Giovanni's* the third mate on a Sicilian fishing trawler."

"You're being nasty as well as absolutely unfair," Jean said angrily. "A lot of people live perfectly good, happy lives without knowing about *Don Giovanni,* or Mozart, for that matter."

"Yes'm lots of good people live without appreciating a Rembrandt, without enjoying Keats or Robert Frost, without losing themselves in a good book or a fine play or a lot of other things. Only not once you've known these things. Once you've known them they become a part of you, and you can't live without them anymore than you can live without breathing. And especially you, girl. They're inside you, and you bubble with them."

"Have you any more words of wisdom for me?" she asked tartly. The fact that her ice-coated tone didn't ruffle his calm assurance made her that much angrier.

"That's about it," he grinned at her. "Except that I learned that your friend Hobart Weatherby controls the town bank. And he owns the general store."

"So?" she frowned. Ted's lips pursed.

"Nothing, I guess. I just thought you'd like knowing the Weatherbys are pretty well fixed. Silent strength versus the sound of money and all that sort of thing," he said coolly.

"Ted Holbrook, you can leave if you're through," she said angrily.

"I was just going," he said, patting her on the top of the head. "Don't glower so," he said from the door, "it causes wrinkles."

She stood listening to him drive off and stalked to her room. Undressing, she slipped into the bed still turning Ted's visit over in her mind. There was more to it than the barbed darts he tossed at Ferris, though that had been more than enough. He'd hit where it hurt, and she hated him for it, but then he always had a talent for knowing where to strike. He was still trying to help her in his own way, she knew, unable to realize that cleverness and words didn't count anymore. Still, there'd been an undertone to his words that clung to her, one more unresolved note to add to the others. She turned on her side and went to sleep quickly, her body still in need of rest. She slept soundly and well until the sound woke her. She snapped her eyes open and lay still, trying to locate it, a thumping noise, then a dragging sound, not unlike the sounds she'd heard that first night in the storm. But there was no undulating call this time to mingle with the wind's howl, only the scraping and the thumping Sitting up, she realized it was coming from directly above her and, frowning, she also realized Fiona MacFie's bedroom was the room over hers. Suddenly, as she had that first night, she felt the pull on her, the need to investigate the strange noises. The scrape dragged over the floor again, the thumps following in quick succession. It sounded like an animal scurrying about and, once again, she thought how an animal could have easily entered the house. *Go and see,* a voice hammered in her head. *Find out. Go and see.*

Jean forced herself back down and let her hands clutch the sides of the bed as she held herself there, her arms rigid. She heard the sound of her breathing, hard, frightened, as she fought against the urge to get up and investigate. As she lay there, listening to the sounds from the room above, she felt her arms hurting from the pressure she held the bed with, and she almost cried out as one arm cramped on her. As she released her grip in pain the sounds suddenly halted, and she lay on her side, rubbing the muscles of her forearm, listening. But there were no more sounds, and she sprawled on her back, feeling her body slowly relax. The moment had passed, and she'd fought down the call that had pulled at her. She fell asleep again, too tired to think any further, as the first light of the new day crept across the sea.

When she woke, Jean dressed and went into the hallway, halting at the bottom of the stairs. Gathering her courage, she mounted the steps, moving quickly, more quickly than she had the first time she'd investigated what secrets the second floor held. She went down the hallway and as she reached the last room, Fiona MacFie's room, she saw the door was ajar. Jean recalled closing the door again behind her when she had left that day. But an animal could have clawed it open. She pulled it open further and entered the room, smelling its dank stuffiness again.

There was nothing different than the last time she'd been there. She breathed a deep sigh. It had to have been an animal. She was turning to leave when a flash of silver caught her eye beside the leg of the old dresser. She bent down and pulled out the faded daguerreotype in the silver frame and stared at it in the palm of her hand. She had put the picture back in and closed the dresser drawer. An animal could have clawed the door open. No animal could have opened the dresser drawer, taken out the picture and reclosed the drawer.

Feeling the strange chill wrap itself around her once again, Jean opened the drawer and put the picture of Fiona MacFie back inside it. She pushed the drawer shut and walked from the room, pushing the door closed after her, trying not to tremble. Had she gone up in the night, had she answered the noises, death would have struck again at her. She was certain of it now, just as she was certain that no animal had been in that room during the night, no animal and no human being. But something had been there, something neither logic nor reason nor Ted Holbrook's pointed skepticism could explain away.

When she reached the bottom of the stairs, Jean leaned her forehead against the wall and waited for her knees to regain their strength. Death wore more than one face here, she told herself, and she would see them both again.

She went outside and sat by the edge of the land, peering over the sea. The fishing trawlers would have passed by hours ago, in the early dawn light. Later, when they returned, she would go to town and find Ferris. She wanted to be with him again, talk to him, feel his presence beside her. Suddenly it was very important to do that. A tiny but persistent thought prodded her, but she refused to listen to it. Ted Holbrook's barbed words had nothing to do with it, she told herself. Absolutely nothing whatever. The ringing of the phone took her back into the house. It was Bob.

"Wanted to get you before you went off doing things," he said. "You're going to let me know what you're up to, remember."

"Yes, I remember," she said. His concern was a warming thing. "I want to go to the boatyard and pay Mr. Thompson for the loss of his boat."

"I can pick you up midafternoon," he said. "I've some things to go over with Dad, first."

"That'll be fine," she said. She hung up glad to have the companionship. She didn't relish going into town alone, not until the atmosphere changed.

The morning passed quickly enough. Amantha arrived late, and Jean stayed outside in the sun, taking the opportunity to wear shorts and a halter. She changed into a skirt and blouse when Bob arrived and they drove into town. The boatyard operator was fair enough, but it still pretty thoroughly depleted Jean's checking account. "How about that dinner with my father?" Bob asked as they started from town. "He does want to talk to you about the fishing rights, especially after what happened the other night."

"Tomorrow evening?" Jean suggested.

"Fine," Bob said, his wide face wider with a happy grin. "I'll pick you up, of course."

The car had just reached the top of the hill that led from town when Jean heard the church bell begin to ring. It rang out solemnly, one deep mournful clang after another in slow, measured cadence. She hadn't noticed the church in town but now, looking back down at the cluster of buildings, she saw the spire tucked away in the far corner of the village. The bell continued to clang, slowly, ominously, and Jean looked at Bob, her brow furrowed.

"That's no late-afternoon ringing of the church bell," she said. "What's it mean?"

"Something's happened at sea," he said, glancing at his watch. "The trawlers have just come in. That's the tolling for the dead." Jean's eyes reflected the shock that passed through her frame. He had turned onto the dune road, and they were at the house in a few minutes.

"I want to find out what happened," she said, the mournful sound of the tolling bell still carrying to the house on a north wind.

"I've got to go to Purdy's Cove on business," Bob said. "I'll phone you when I get back and find out what happened. It mightn't be till early evening."

"Soon as you can," she said, and Bob drove away quickly. The tolling bell, faint but clear, continued for another fifteen minutes before stopping. When it did, Jean saw Amantha, her coat on, going out the door, and she followed the woman outside.

"Why so early, Amantha?" she asked.

"You heard the bell," the woman said. "There'll be trouble. I'm not staying."

"What kind of trouble?" Jean questioned. The big woman shrugged. "Trouble," she said and hurried away. Jean watched her go up the hill and disappear where the footpath led between the rocks. Turning, the girl went back into the house and felt its chill, tomblike silence wrap around her. She shook her shoulders and made some soup from a package she found in the kitchen. Some crackers she uncovered added to it, and that did as supper. Her stomach wasn't much for eating, and she thought of trying to reach Ted. No doubt he'd know what had happened. She found the number of the only place listed as taking in guests and dialed it. A voice told her that Mr. Holbrook was out, and she hung up the phone in more than annoyance. The night had settled itself, and Jean went to the door to look out. It was clear, and the wind was cold. She had just started to shut the door when she saw the figure appear at the top of the rocks, half-over the edge of the land. Even in the night she recognized the powerful chest, the wide shoulders, and she rushed outside. She was in his arms at the edge of the rocks, feeling his hands dig into her shoulders.

"Get away from here, Jean," he said. "They're coming, they're past control." His voice was tense with urgency.

"Who?" she asked.

"Most everyone," he said. "A tanker rammed the *Mary II* today. Young Sutherland and the Allrich boy were killed. They're blaming you for it. If the cove had been open to us, it wouldn't have happened. They're coming here to burn the house down and drive you from it. If you don't go they'll burn it down with you in it. They're ugly, Jean."

The old house wasn't worth saving, certainly not getting killed for, and yet she couldn't run. "I'm not going," she said simply. "I'll tell them I'll open the cove."

"They won't believe you," Ferris said. "They'll say it's more words, more trying to delay things."

Jean pressed herself against the big man. "I'll make them listen to me," she said.

"No, it won't work," he said. "They're out for vengeance." She grimaced. Vengeance. It was a word she'd come to know well. Ferris held her arms with his huge hands and looked deep into her eyes. "I got away and ran here," he said. "I've got to get back before they start looking for me. If they knew I was here they'd have done with me, too. Leave, Jean, leave now, before it's too late for me to help you."

She circled his oaklike neck with her arms and found his lips. "Thank you for trying, Ferris," she whispered to him. He drew away, his eyes burning into her, his face grave, and then he was gone, clambering down the rocks with the speed and surefootedness of a mountain goat.

"Idiocy. Plain, unvarnished idiocy," she heard the voice say, and she whirled to see Ted's lanky form emerge from the shadows of the house.

"Are you adding eavesdropping to your other talents?" she said, eyes blazing.

"Sorry about that," he said. "But you were so involved you didn't even hear me drive up. I didn't want to interrupt that touching little scene. Come on, I'll get you out of here."

"No," she said. "I'm staying."

"That's lunacy," he said. "I just came from town. That's a mob down there, and you can't reason with a mob. Laughing Boy was right. They're out for vengeance."

"Don't you see, Ted, I can't go. I've told you that. It's more than just being logical. I had to come here and I have to stay. Isn't that proof enough of what I've been telling you?"

"No, dammit," he shouted back. "It's proof that you've got yourself so wound up that you're self-hypnotized. You've got maybe a half hour before they start coming. Are you going with me or not?"

"You just can't see it, can you, Ted?"

"I see I've got better things to do than stay here arguing with you," he said. "Good luck, Jeanie girl. I'm not sticking around here."

He turned and ran to the car, driving off with a shower of dirt flung back at her by the spinning wheels. She turned away, not blaming him. He had tried in his own way. It was wrong to ask him to be something he wasn't. Jean went into the house, walking slowly. She had come here to find answers she had thought, and now she knew she had come here for many reasons. Perhaps it was only fitting that the answers she wanted should come, not through quiet contemplation, but through pain, not through reason and logic, but through strange forces yet unknown.

Inside the hall she took the hurricane lamp and went up the stairs. But on the second floor she didn't go down the long hall, turning instead to the wall along the front end of the house until she found the doorway. Pulling it open she stepped out onto the narrow widow's walk, gingerly touching the swaying and rotted railing. She could see the dim white of the beach and a good stretch of the dune road, a faint ribbon under the low moon. As she stood there looking out to sea, as Fiona MacFie stood there over a century ago, she felt the wind on her face, and she waited, the minutes ticking silently off. A half hour had gone by since Ferris had hurried off into the night. Suddenly she heard the first, low rumble of voices. She looked out into the night and saw the lights, some flickering, others, the steady beams of flashlights. Some men were coming up the beach, some along the dune road, and as she watched them approach she saw those in the foreground carrying improvised torches. She saw them converging on the house, some clambering up the rocks, some over the sand dunes, and the main group coming down the dune road.

Jean looked down at the mob as they gathered in front of the house, able to see only that some were women. The torchlight and the dark made picking out Ferris impossible.

"Listen to me, please!" Jean shouted to them. "This is wrong. I want to help you!"

"We've seen enough of that!" a voice shouted in answer.

"Burn it down! Set the torch to it!" another shout cut the night.

"Please listen to me!" Jean implored.

"No more talk!" a voice answered. "No more lies! No more stalling while we die!"

More angry shouts joined the chorus, and Jean looked down at the angry, arm-waving mob. Was one of those voices that of the killer that had stalked her in the fog? One of the mob below her had carefully planned her death that night. Maybe more than one had been in on it, and she felt her own stubborn anger rising.

"I'm not moving from here," she shouted defiantly, glad they could not see how tightly her hands were clasped atop the weathered wood railing.

"Don't let her bluff you!" a voice shouted. "Let's go! Put the torch to the house!"

Jean glanced nervously back into the house. The dry old place would go into roaring flames at once. The front exits would be almost instantly blocked by flames. Would she have time to get out the back? Were they clogged and jammed or boarded up?

"Please listen to me!" she shouted again. "I'm going to see that the cove is opened for fishing."

"Don't believe her!" someone shouted. "That's just more talk!"

The crowd surged forward, individual voices merging in a chorus of shouts, angry, unreasoning sounds. Jean turned from the rail and halted as the shot exploded the night, a powerful, heavy, shotgun blast. She heard the crowd halt and angry voices fall into silence, and she turned to peer out into the night. The voice rose from the right side of the dune road, on a small rise of a rock.

"Hold on, friends," the voice said, and Jean's eyes widened with astonishment. Along with the others, she turned to see the tall figure with the rifle in his hand. A young boy, not more than twelve, stood alongside him.

"It can't be!" she murmured aloud, her voice a gasping whisper. But it was, the unruly lock of hair falling over his forehead, the clear voice, soft for all its clarity.

"Ted!" she exclaimed again in a whisper. "Ted!"

She was still open-mouthed as the tall figure spoke again to the crowd.

"You've got ten minutes to go back to town and forget this whole business," Ted was saying. "If you don't, you'll have nothing to fish with in the cove or anywhere else. There are two sticks of dynamite on the foredeck of each of your trawlers. Each one has a fuse with about ten minutes burning time."

"Who's he?" someone shouted, finding his voice. "He's trying to scare us," someone else said.

"I anticipated you'd think that so I brought this boy with me. You all know him, I'm sure. His name's Timmy," Ted said.

"He's telling the truth," the boy shouted. "I saw him do it."

"You've got about eight minutes left now," Ted said calmly.

The crowd muttered, swayed, and then broke, those in the rear leading the way as they turned and started to race back toward town. In moments they were gone, every one of them, streaming away in the distance. Jean stepped from the walkway, and inside the house she ran down the steps, almost falling in her haste. She reached the bottom step as Ted entered, holding the shotgun in his hand. He walked into the library and sprawled across a chair. Jean moved toward him, her lips parted, her eyes still incredulous saucers. He tossed a grin at her.

"Surprised, eh?" he commented. "I'm a little surprised myself. I think it's called rising to the occasion."

"Yes, I'd say it certainly was. I really don't know quite what to say, Ted," Jean stammered.

"There was a supply and equipment store and I saw the dynamite sticks and got the idea. Bought the shotgun there, too."

"What if they come back?"

"They won't. Not tonight, anyway. The mood's been broken."

Jean surveyed the long, hazel-eyed face. The cool, almost detached expression remained as always, but in his eyes she saw a new note, a hint of grimness she had never seen there before. Easing herself into a straight-backed chair, she peered at Ted with a frown, still hardly able to believe what she had seen. As if to accommodate her, he quickly proceeded to show her that he was not that changed.

"I expected a bit more from Mount Rushmore," he commented blandly. "I mean, after all, he was out there somewhere."

"He came here to warn me," Jean protested. "He risked his place in the community, his work, perhaps his life. He was helpless to do more. He was trapped, caught between his own people and me."

"Terrible," Ted clucked. "All that silent, inner strength tied up in knots." Jean tried to hold back her glare. "There's a moral in that somewhere," he added with a bright smile. "A little weakness is good for the character."

He was back being his old, cutting, irritatingly assured self again and enjoying it as always. Any other time she'd have snapped back at him. Now she felt guilty about her glare. The phone rang, and she got up to take it. She heard Bob's voice, agitated, concerned. "I just got back," he said. "Passing through town we heard the talk about what happened. Thank God, you're all right. I'll be by tomorrow."

She heard the quiver in his voice. His care for her was more than casual, and she had respect for that. Never again would she lightly treat the gift of caring, and she hung up with the warm feeling Bob always managed to leave with her.

Ted's eyes were cool, narrowed, as she returned to her chair.

"By the way, I found out that old man Weatherby owns the gasoline station that fuels the fishing fleet," he said. "He owns the local variety store, too. He seems to own most of the town."

"What are you trying to tell me?" Jean asked.

"I'm not sure myself," Ted said, and his eyes narrowed for a brief instant, and then the cool casualness was on him again. "Footnotes for future consideration, I guess," he commented. Getting up suddenly, he pulled Jean to her feet, brushed her forehead with his lips and walked to the door. "I'll be around in the morning, Jeanie girl," he said. "Get some sleep."

It was good advice, and after he'd gone she tumbled into bed, not bothering with a nightgown, letting the cool sheets caress her body. She felt drained, the reaction of her fear returning to take its toll. Her sleep was fitful again, and the night was less than half-finished when she was wakened, the reddish glow lighting the window. She leaped from bed and ran to the glass. The ghostly light was moving across the sea again, from Rock Island, the shapeless, eerie glow that was the ghost of Fiona MacFie's bridal boat. She stood transfixed, watching the glow until it simply vanished into the air as it had the other times. As she climbed back into bed she knew that nothing had been changed by what had happened earlier in the evening. None of the questions had been answered, and she knew she must still find those answers. Or, she shuddered as she closed her eyes, tomorrow would be forever unfinished.

CHAPTER SEVEN

The phone call to Hobart Weatherby was Jean's first act after she'd finished dressing. The decision had been with her when she wakened and she saw no point in waiting to discuss it further over dinner. The man's voice was smoothly agreeable and she was grateful for that.

"You'll advise the fishermen that the cove is open to them," Jean said. "I don't want to wait for the government report."

"Whatever you wish, my dear," Hobart Weatherby answered. "We'll see to everything."

"Thank you," Jean said and hung up quickly. She stepped from the library to see Ted leaning in the doorway.

"I just told Hobart Weatherby to open the cove for fishing," she said.

"So much for that," Ted commented. "You ready?"

"To do what?"

"To pack it in," he said. "To hie ourselves back to the warmer climes. I said I'd come by this morning."

"I didn't know that's what you meant, Ted," Jean said. "I'm not leaving Hawk's End yet. I can't. The questions aren't answered for me yet. Last night, I saw the burning bridal boat again, that glow at sea I told you about. It was there. I didn't imagine it."

"It was there, all right. I saw it, too," Ted said, and Jean's eyes widened. "But it's sure as hell not what you think it is or what that old legend says it is," he went on. "I called an old friend last night after I saw the damn thing from my room, woke him out of bed, in fact. He's a professor of natural sciences at MIT. I explained what I'd seen and that it's been seen often. He took an educated guess from what I told him and said it was probably a phenomenon of the northern lights, the aurora borealis. You're plenty far enough north here for them to be seen. I couldn't get all the technical stuff he tossed at me, but it had something to do with an image reflection bouncing off clouds at certain times and reflecting onto the water in concentrated focus."

"It has to be that way for you, doesn't it?" Jean said. "It doesn't explain away all the other things that have happened, the things I feel inside me, but you've got to clutch at a reason you can understand."

"The things you feel inside you you've put there yourself, Jeanie," Ted said, his eyes dark with anger.

"Have I, Ted?" she answered. "Have I?"

"Yes, dammit! You want it this way. Maybe that cackling witch of a housekeeper is right about you being possessed. You're possessed by guilt feelings about Evan, and they're so big they've taken over the way you think, the way you feel, and just about everything else. You had them when you went off by yourself and now they're worse."

"Don't you believe in anything but the things you can see and touch and explain in practical terms?"

"Yes, but not these things," Ted shot back.

"Please, Ted, try to understand," she pleaded.

"No, thanks, doll. I've had it," he bit out. "There's a helluva storm coming this way according to the weather reports. It's due tomorrow, and I don't intend to be here when it hits. You can stick around here and chase your burning ghost ships and play tag with old Fiona MacFie's spirit and keep on finding the wrong reasons for everything that happens. Me, I'm bowing out, here and now. I've got a date with a dry martini."

"Ted!" Jean called out as he whirled and disappeared through the doorway.

"Tell it to Mount Rushmore," she heard him fling back, and she made herself stand still, listening to the angry roar of the car engine speeding away. She wanted to run after him but she didn't. He had done enough and shown her another side of him, perhaps found it here himself and that was all to the good. It was better this way. It was hers and hers alone to wrestle with. She'd been the one to step on the gift. She should be the one to pay if payment had to be made.

The girl turned and started toward her room. Amantha hadn't appeared and was obviously not coming today. The house seemed emptier than it had ever been. She could feel the malevolence of its silent triumph. As she reached the room she heard the sound of a car stopping outside, and she whirled and ran to the door, hoping to see the little dark green MG. She kept the disappointment from showing on her face as she saw Bob.

"I came to take you for a drive," he said. "Anywhere, just to get you out of this old place."

The idea appealed at once, and she was touched by the depth of his concern. His hand on her elbow, helping her into the car, was reassuring. It reminded her that before the storm came to close down the land she must see Ferris and borrow strength from him, enough to last her a little while longer.

"I know your father doesn't agree with my decision," she said to Bob as they drove west around the edge of the land. "But I don't want to be a part in any more lives being lost."

"It's all being taken care of," Bob said, dismissing the subject. "You just forget about everything and relax."

She nodded, putting her head back against the seat and watching the sea slowly building, its blue turning gray under fast-moving clouds. Bob drove for hours, letting her relax, talking hardly at all, and she was grateful for his sensitivity. By the time they had completed a huge circle and returned to the house, the day was drawing to a close, and the sea was gray green with winds racing along the rising waves. Rock Island rose in the distance, a grim reminder of how close death had come, a tantalizing source of ghostly lights in the night.

Bob's hand was on her arm as she started to swing from the car, his eyes concerned under a frown.

"Check in with me tonight. I'll feel better," he said. She nodded, and he leaned over to kiss her cheek. He was nice, thoroughly nice, she concluded as she watched him drive off; none of the magnetic strength that was in Ferris Duncan, but a quiet dependability of his own. Her lips tightened as, from nowhere, Ted's words flashed in front of her. Silent strength versus the sound of money, he had said. Damn that Ted Holbrook, she grimaced. His way with a phrase hung on like a persistent cold. She went into the silent house and heard the wood already creak as the wind pulled at it. The sea was still gathering itself, she saw. It would be another twelve hours before it was in all its screaming, wind-driven fury, she estimated. She wondered if she could stay another stormy night alone in the old house, and she was glad again for Bob's invitation to call him. She might ask him for refuge. She straightened her shoulders and walked to her room. The note propped up atop the dresser caught her eye at once, and she opened it quickly.

> Important for you that you meet me at cove, by the landing. Seven o'clock.
>
> Amantha

Jean frowned at the cryptic note. The woman must have uncovered something important. She was not the kind for writing notes. Had she learned who had tried to kill her in the fog that night? But why the cove? Perhaps she had found the evidence there. Jean pushed the note into her skirt pocket and glanced at her watch. She had a little over an hour to wait, and she made herself a cup of tea and watched the night move in from the sea. The surf was crashing onto the beach with increasing fury as she left the house, her flashlight in hand, and hurried along the narrow path toward the cove. The wind clutched at her, whipping her skirt up to reveal her long, lithe legs.

At the edge of the slope that led down to the cove she took hold of the rocks and scrubby brush, lowering herself carefully until she was on the small rocky beach that rimmed the cove. An intermittent moon, peering between the fast-moving clouds, showed her the sea striking the land, not with its full force, but with strength enough to toss small rocks up onto the shorefront. She heard a noise, like that of a foot striking a rock, and she spun around, shining her light toward it. "Amantha?" she called, but there was no answer. She had just flicked off the light when the blow struck her from behind, coming down hard on the back of her neck. She pitched forward, the flashlight falling from her hand, and her head throbbing with a dull ache. She felt the hardness of the small rocks and pebbles as she landed on her face. She tried to turn but a hand came down over her mouth, an arm around her neck. Her own hand, outstretched on the rocky floor of the shoreline, closed around a sharp-edged, flat stone. She brought it around and raked the edge of it across the hand that was clamping her mouth shut, slamming it down with desperate strength.

She heard the muffled exclamation of pain, a muttered oath and the hand was pulled away. She felt the fleck of blood strike her face. Trying to turn her head, she was yanked to her feet. Another blow came down, this one striking hard on her head. She felt her legs dissolve, the world spin, and then she was being flung into the water. She went under at once, shaking her head, conscious enough to keep her mouth closed. Her attacker was waiting on the edge of the shore, she knew, ready to strike again if she were able to crawl out of the water. She let herself stay down, swimming automatically, and her hand brushed against something hard, long, and she curled an arm around one of the supports of the narrow landing. Her lungs aflame, she let herself rise and found three or four inches of air space under the boards of the dock. As she hung there, gulping in air, treading water, she could see the beam of her flashlight sweeping the water, searching for signs of her body. She didn't dare move from beneath the dock, and she saw the cold-white beam of the flashlight pass over the boards and move along the water. Her attacker methodically swept the water with the light, first one way then the other, back and forth. Then, as she heard the footsteps on the boards of the landing, she let herself sink under the surface, keeping one hand against the post. The flashlight played across the water from the end of the landing, and then the attacker walked back to the land. Jean rose to drink in the air, her head pressed against the undersides of the boards.

The flashlight beam no longer moved across the water but she stayed in her hiding place, holding the support post against the wind-driven water that tried to push her out into the open. Her would-be killer could still be there, waiting, making certain, and she'd take no chances. Was it the assailant who'd tried to kill her in the fog at sea, she wondered. Had Amantha deliberately led her into the trap? Or was Amantha her attacker? She had held the thought once and had discarded it, but she could discard it no longer. She let almost an hour go by, and she was shivering with the cold as she softly moved from under the boards of the long, narrow landing, pausing at the edge to scan the narrow pebbled border of the cove.

Nothing moved, and the only sound was the sound of the water and the rushing wind. She swam the few feet to the shoreline and climbed out of the water, pausing again to wait and listen. But the attacker had gone, convinced the deed had been accomplished. As she pulled herself up the steep slope, shivering in the night wind, she thought again about Amantha. Perhaps the attacker had known Amantha had learned something and had followed her to the cove. Perhaps he had killed the big, gaunt-faced woman already and then lain in wait for Jean. Reaching the top of the slope, Jean ran toward the house, reaching it and slamming the door shut behind her, leaning against it and letting her breath return in deep, sobbing gasps. The attack in the boat had been by one of the fishermen, she'd been certain. But why now, after she had opened the cove? Perhaps Hobart Weatherby hadn't notified them yet. Or perhaps this attack tonight was pure vengeance, hate over those who'd been killed in the collision at sea, an eye for an eye. The possibilities seemed to multiply the more she thought about them, and she ran to her room, flinging off her soaked clothing to put on slacks and a jacket over a blouse.

Running to the library, she phoned Bob and almost sobbed as his calm voice answered.

"Jean?" he said.

"Yes, you told me to call, remember?"

"Of course," he said quickly. "I just somehow expected you'd call later, before going to bed."

"No," she said. "No, I want to leave here, now." Words falling over each other, she told him what had happened, and when she'd finished she heard his voice, patient, calm.

"I'll come right over," he said. "You wait there. It's as safe as anywhere for you. My engine's been acting up so it may take a few minutes longer but you wait there."

"All right," she said. "Thank you, Bob. Hurry."

She put down the phone and went back to her room, lying down on the bed, keeping her body from trembling. The wind was rising steadily, blowing in fits and starts, and she could hear the surf crashing onto the beach. She had wanted a hard lonely place, uncompromising, unyielding. She had wanted to find herself, to find answers, to discover what was meaningful and real in life. Instead, she had discovered the unreal, strange forces that clutched and held the soul, and the only reality was the reality of death. She'd come to punish herself, Ferris Duncan had said that first day. She lived in her own guilt, Ted had said, and perhaps they were both right.

She lay quietly, waiting, letting the minutes tick off. He was late, she told herself grimly. As she lay there she felt her skin grow cold, and she sat up. She was no longer alone in the old house. It was as it had been that first night she'd come here to the house at Hawk's End, when she'd wakened before the fire and knew she was not alone. It was the same and yet different. She'd broken into a cold perspiration that night and felt the presence of something she couldn't explain in the house. Now she felt only terror, fear of the real, not the unreal. She heard the sound, faint, of a door being pushed open on old hinges. The sound came from the very rear of the house, and she edged from her room, running on tiptoe to the library. She would phone Bob and learn how long ago he'd left. She lifted the phone carefully and held it to her ear. It was silent as a tomb. Hands of ice wrapped around her heart as she put the receiver back on the cradle. The wires had been cut, and she heard the creak of a floorboard, of footsteps moving across the floor. Only the lamp in the library was on, and she blew it out, plunging the house into total darkness.

Her attacker at the cove must have seen her as she returned to the house and had lain in wait, making certain there was no one in the house with her and no one coming. Oh, God, Bob, hurry, hurry, she murmured to herself. Please hurry! The floorboard creaked again in the silent house, closer this time. He had seen her blow out the lamp and knew she was in the library. She had to move or be trapped there, she realized. She heard the sound, still closer, and she darted out of the room, diving across the foyer. She saw the figure, a dim shape in the darkness, lunge for her, and she flung herself to the left. Hands clutched at her, and she saw the long rain slicker. She pushed hard with both hands, knocking her attacker off-balance, and then she was out the door, racing into the night. She paused to peer down the dune road for headlights but the road was black. *My engine's been acting up.* She heard his words, and they hung bitterly in the wind. Behind her she heard the door flung open, and she saw the tall figure, the rain slicker gray white in the dark, moving after her. She would have to run. If Bob came he'd search for her. Jean turned, cast a frantic glance at the beach. Not there, it was too open. The land on the other side of the dune road rose in brush and tough grass and rocks. She ran, terror giving her speed she did not ordinarily possess.

She saw a rocky rise and the brush above, and she ran for it, glimpsing the figure coming from behind. The low clouds were still patchwork, and they let the moon scatter its cold light for brief moments. She hid in the shadow of a rock as the moon lighted the scene for an instant and then, when it went out, she ran again. The figure was gaining, his footsteps closer. Her hand skidded off a boulder and, as the stone moved, she fell to one knee. The pursuing figure heard her, and looking back, she saw it change direction and come up the side of the rise. Jean leaped up behind the loose stone. Putting her back against it and pressing, she sent it toppling and took a second to see her pursuer dive to one side as the stone rolled directly at him. He had avoided being hit, but his pursuit had been slowed and even a few seconds helped. She was running again, taking every small rocky path that appeared. Suddenly, she saw a passageway to the left, between rounded rocks and to one side of a clump of brush with a fallen tree. She dived into the brush, wriggling herself beneath the fallen tree trunk like a rabbit running from a fox. The brush was thick and she felt it close over her as she lay hidden there, hardly daring to breathe.

Her attacker's footsteps sounded, then halted, and she heard his heavy breathing. His? Hers? It was impossible to tell, but something in the way her pursuer moved made her almost certain it wasn't Amantha. The big woman, for all her size and strength, had an awkwardness about her. Jean listened, her face pressed into the thick roots of the brush, and she heard the figure move on. But how far? Was he waiting, too? The hunt was often a matter of matching patience, and this was indeed a hunt with death waiting to claim her at the close of it. She shifted position, a fraction of an inch at a time, and then lay quiet again, listening. He had made one mistake at the cove. He was not going to make another if he could help it, she knew.

Had Bob come and found her gone? He must have by now, she reasoned, and he would be frantically searching for her. But of course he wouldn't hunt up here amid the rocks and tangled brush. He'd look for her in town and call the police. She snorted to herself. She doubted that Hawk's End had a police force. She was about to risk a move when she heard the soft clatter of small stones as they rolled down an embankment. Her pursuer was above somewhere, watching for a sign of her, certain she hadn't outdistanced him. His foot had dislodged the little trail of pebbles, probably as he shifted position. Her throat was dry and she could tell the wind was blowing harder by the movement of the brush as it tugged against her. She knew that hours had gone by and the first light of dawn would be filtering down through the clouds soon. She had to make a move. In the daylight, even the dawn, gray with a coming storm, her body would be quickly spotted through the loose brush, especially from above.

She would have to run for it again, somehow get away from him and get to town. There she could find Ferris or phone Bob. Once that was done the tables would be turned. Her attacker's right hand bore deep gashes where she had raked it with the sharp stone. He wouldn't be hard to spot. Carefully, Jean lifted herself up, pushing her body through the brush as she sat up. Above her she could see smooth rock and clumps of brush and ledges. He was up there someplace, listening more than looking. In the still, dark hillside, ears were better than eyes. She saw a piece of the fallen tree, rotted away, a section about three feet long and half a foot deep. Leaning sideways with care, she could reach it. She picked up the length of wood, lifted it over her head, and flung it with all her might to the left. She dropped back into the brush as the wood struck into a side of rock, then thumped and clattered its way down the hill. She heard the racing footsteps almost at once as her pursuer gave chase to the sound he thought was her leaping down the hillside.

She pushed herself to her feet at once and ran upwards and then, on a ledge that seemed to go level, across the hillside, glimpsing the dune road below through a crack in the rocks and shifting her course to head down for it. He had, of course, discovered she had tricked him by now, but she had gained time and distance and, more importantly, shaken him off her trail. Moving sideways as she ran, pausing for breath only when she had to, she made her way down to the dune road, and at the end of it, the shorter hill that led down to the sleeping town. The grayness of the day tinted the sky as she ran into the town, hearing her footsteps on the cobbled street as she raced past the piers where the trawlers were tied fast, battened down with heavy tarpaulins for the coming storm. At the end of the street that runs along the water, Ferris had said. Her breath coming in harsh gasps, she stopped at a railing that bordered the stone of the low seawall. There were only two buildings left on the street, the first a warehouse, the second a small, frame building. Pushing herself from the rail, she ran forward and fell against the open doorway of the small building. She saw the name FERRIS DUNCAN written over the top of one of three doorbells, and she pressed a finger on the button. She heard the bell ringing, just beyond the front door on the ground floor. Seconds later a door opened and Ferris stepped into the hall. He was fully dressed. Fishing boats usually set out with the dawn tide, she knew.

His handsomely rugged face clouded as he saw her and he came forward quickly, reaching toward her. She saw the neat, white strip of bandage across his right hand. The world stopped moving for an instant, and she forgot to breathe. She stared at the hand and then, shock and fear mingling in her eyes, she looked up at Ferris as he came toward her. She felt herself backing away, words hard to get out.

"Your hand," she gasped.

"A gash from a fishhook," the big man said. His deep eyes were penetrating.

"The bandage is brand-new," she breathed, still backing away, feeling the street under her feet now.

"I just put on a fresh one," he said. "What is it?" he asked, and he moved quickly, reaching out for her. The world exploded and she heard her own voice half-shouting, half-sobbing.

"No. Oh, God, no!" she was saying, and she turned and ran, back the way she'd come.

"Come back here!" she heard him shout, and she looked back to see him start after her. Turning, she saw the tall figure in the rain slicker appear at the far end of the street. Not just one killer, she heard herself murmur silently. They had plotted, maybe even drawn straws, and Ferris had been among them. The tall figure stepped behind the building line but she had glimpsed him, and she turned down a narrow alleyway between two buildings. It led her to another street, winding and narrow. Looking north she saw the raincoated figure come into view, running now, coming after her, and she turned and ran, following the curve of the street. She glanced back to see the figure cut into another side alley as Ferris, closer to her, emerged from the alleyway she had taken. They were going to try to cut her off.

"Jean, come here!" It was Ferris's voice, and she almost stopped. What if he'd told her the truth? What if he had gashed his hand on a fishhook? But what if he hadn't, she asked herself at once. She couldn't risk it. She had called death to her once before in the fogbound sea. She wouldn't do it again. Running, she crossed a small triangle of three converging streets and saw the man in the raincoat starting down one. She could hear Ferris's footsteps behind her and she switched directions, racing down a short street and back to the waterfront. The little boatyard was just beyond here someplace, she remembered and as she emerged onto the waterfront street she saw the small collection of tired old outboards just ahead. She'd eluded them both for a moment but she knew it was only a moment. The wharf was deserted in the early gray light, and she took off her shoes as she reached it, running across the boards on silent feet. Halting beside a dory with an outboard, almost identical to the one she had rented, she dropped into it and peered over the edge of the wharf. She saw Ferris emerge onto the street, look around, and then start up in the opposite direction. But he'd be back, she knew. The other one hadn't appeared yet but he was no doubt, waiting in the dark of a doorway someplace.

Jean peered ahead of her, at the open sea. In the distance she saw the barely visible dark gray blur that was Rock Island. Behind her were men trying to kill her. Behind her were reasons she neither knew nor understood and now, suddenly, she knew what she had to do. She was being called again, by a voice she couldn't hear, yet had to obey, a voice she had come to know in all its silent strength, a voice that seemed to be calling her home. Rock Island was suddenly more than a place of legends and curiosity, more than a refuge, a hiding place from her pursuers. It would be, she knew with a certainty that was more than hers, a place of answers. A feeling of finality wrapped itself around her, as if threads were being pulled together from many places.

Rising carefully from the bottom of the dory, she scanned the wave-tossed little harbor. She could clear it in a matter of minutes and be on her way. Beyond the harbor the sea would be rising in remorseless fury, she knew, but the sturdy dory could still ride the waves. All she needed was an hour or two of safety, enough time for the boatyard owner to find his dory missing and for Bob to put two and two together. He'd come after her then, and she'd be waiting on Rock Island with answers; answers she knew she could only find there. Once again she felt the wave of excitement course through her body. It had begun with the call that had come to her in the dead of night, waking her with its urgency, an urgency that went unrecognized then, and now it would end with the raging storm beating against her, another kind of urgency, somehow so terribly fitting.

Crawling forward, Jean slipped the bowline from the bolard, glancing back at the quay. She heard footsteps in the gray morning mist as the boat slid slowly from the dock. They'd hear her go off, of course, but she counted on them not following. They'd hope the sea would do what they had failed to do. If she merely headed out to sea, it would certainly do just that, but she had a destination, a date with her own, clouded, stormy destiny. And even if they thought she headed for the island, it was a good wager they'd not follow after her. Killers or not, they lived with a hundred years of superstition.

Jean yanked the starter and the sound seemed to explode in the silence. The motor caught at once and, she swung the dory to starboard and headed out of the harbor, past the short curved breakwater and into the sea, uttering a short, silent prayer for Bob to pick up her trail as quickly as possible. The moment she cleared the breakwater the sea caught the little dory, lifting it high, then plunging it into deep troughs where all she could see were walls of towering green. The sea was nasty, she saw, nastier than she had guessed, and she realized that her timetable for being rescued was far shorter than she had estimated. In a few more hours the sea would be impassable, a towering fury smashing anything that dared to face it.

The dory was light enough to ride the crests and she clung to the tiller, watching each wave carefully, riding up each one with just the right momentum, taking care not to be swept aside and broached, she eyed the windswept clouds filled with rain about to burst on the world. She recalled Ferris's comment on Rock Island. In a bad storm, he had said, the sea sweeps right over it. The sea would be sweeping over it before this one ended, she knew. Cresting a broad wave, she saw Rock Island dead ahead, looming larger now, nothing but rocks jutting up like so many tombstones askew.

She sailed the dory on and over every wave she could crest, the wind blowing spray into her teeth until she tasted salt with every breath. She was a dot on the vast sea, entirely alone, and yet she didn't feel alone at all. Closing onto the shoreline of the island, she felt only an eager anticipation. Churning water to the right told her of the presence of hidden rocks and she steered to port. Dropping speed, she let a wave take her onto the pebbly beach. As it did, the dory capsized and she was tossed into the water, churned up in a rush of spray and flung onto the shore along with the boat. Scrambling to her feet, she ran in beyond the clutch of the water and climbed onto the nearest block of the irregular stones that dotted the island. The dory lay on shore, overturned, but high enough not to be dragged out to sea until the water level rose further. Climbing higher on the rocks, Jean saw that the island was aptly named. It was rock and more rock, with here and there a vestigial bush. Deep cuts ran between some of the stones, and near where she climbed she saw a high-sided cut, half-filled now with the angry sea. In normal weather it would make a perfect dock, just wide enough and long enough to hold a small vessel.

Was this where Aran Connare had prepared his bridal boat to set sail on its last voyage of fiery doom? Did she sit where he had brooded and planned his timeless answer to Fiona MacFie? The wind howled as it whipped through the squared rocks, a cry without end, an anguished screamed turned back upon itself. As she scanned the barren island, a stony retreat of infinite privacy, she knew Fiona and Aran must have come here often. Her eyes roamed the island, looking for what she knew she couldn't find, a worldly echo of something that now existed in another world.

Jean turned her gaze to the sea and saw it was getting nastier more quickly than she'd expected. The waves on the open seaside of the island were shattering with a force that sent spray over the topmost rocks. She had come here to avoid death, to find a refuge. But had that been only a thought given her, another way of calling her to her death? So far she had eluded that final price each time, refusing to satisfy the force that had seized her. Had she eluded it for the last time, she asked herself. It would be the final irony because she had come here to the house at Hawk's End to find herself, to find the meaning and importance in living, and the dead were teaching that to her. Out of yesterday and today they spoke to her of the meaning of love, their voices hard, unforgiving, demanding payment for their lessons.

She turned her head to the left as a gust of wind slammed into the island with extra fury, and her eyes caught the small, bobbing object nearing the shoreline. In astonishment she saw the dory ride in on a huge wave, two men in it, both wearing foul-weather gear. She slipped down to the shoreline and watched the dory come onto the narrow edge of the island. They had done what she was certain they wouldn't do, come after her, defy the hundred years of fear and superstition. She stood still, watching the men pull the dory onto the shore. There was no place to run, no place to hide on this barren bit of land. There was no running for her anymore, no running anywhere again.

The men turned and started toward her and as they did her heart leaped.

"Bob!" she cried out, seeing the familiar face, the wind rushing off with her voice. She leaped down from the rock and ran toward the advancing figures. Bob moved forward to meet her quickly, and she saw Hobart Weatherby following him. His arms caught her, and before her eyes could cloud with shock, she saw the blow arc down at her, felt his hand smash into her face, and she was falling backward, dazed, hitting the pebbled beach. A swirl of cold water struck her face, and her eyes cleared. She looked up at Bob's frowning, angry scowl, at Hobart Weatherby beside him, reaching down for her.

"Meddling little bitch!" the older man said, his words leaping out at her with the force of a whip, slashing into her. His hand half-lifted her to her feet only to send her hurtling to the ground again with another blow that snapped her head halfway around.

The pain and fear were less than the numbing shock, the total incredulousness that had seized her, and the girl lay on the ground, staring up at the two men. Hobart Weatherby's tall figure, looking even taller in the rain slicker, suddenly possessed a frightening familiarity and Jean heard the sound of her breath as it was sucked in sharply.

"The figure in the boat," she gasped. "That night in the fog… it was *you!*"

"You were lucky," Hobart Weatherby snarled at her. "You've been damned lucky all along, but your luck's finally run out."

The absolute incomprehensibility of it engulfed her once again, and she stared from Hobart Weatherby to Bob, his genial face now a scowling, furrowed mask. The questions tumbled from her in desperation as she sought answers before she had neither time nor life left to hear them.

"Everything that happened, then, you were behind it all?" she asked.

"No, we didn't get another chance at you till down at the inlet last night," Weatherby said. "I left the note for you while Bob had you out on that drive in the afternoon."

His words struck at her as though they were physical blows, a confirmation of numbing proportions. All the other times that death had reached out for her rose up before her eyes, the cornerpost that first night, the sounds in the house that had called her to the edge of death, the rock slide, the very summons that had brought her here to Hawk's End and now, that final beckoning that had taken her to Rock Island, all part of one inexorable force. She looked at the two men standing before her and knew that whatever their twisted rationale was for wanting her dead they were, in reality, no more than pawns, unknowingly carrying out the unceasing demands of the dead. It was ironic and she almost smiled. They would kill her and never know of the forces that had brought her here, the combination of yesterday's vengeance and today's retribution. Her thoughts made her stare up at Bob, and she started to pull herself to her feet.

"Why, Bob?" she asked. He had reasons and she would at least hear them. She was halfway up when his hand shot out and smashed against her face, knocking her backward. Before the pain shot through her, she glimpsed the scarred gash along the back of his hand.

"Let's get done with it," she heard him rasp. "This sea's going to be past sailing back in a few minutes."

She looked up through pain-filled, tear-clouded eyes to see Bob drawing back his fist to smash it down on her again, and then she heard Hobart Weatherby's voice.

"Wait, we've got company," he said, and she turned to look out to the sea and the small boat riding a wave onto the shore of the island, a lone figure in it. Ferris, she said silently. It had to be Ferris, and she thought of how she had let fear and panic rob her of reason and faith. And yet, could she have done differently? She got to her feet and started to dart past Hobart Weatherby, but Bob was faster, seizing her, his hand clamping down over her mouth.

"No you don't," he said, dragging her behind one of the squared rocks.

"Ferris, be careful!" she shouted but heard only the muffled, garbled sound of the words as the hand across her mouth held her tightly. She could see, along with the Weatherbys, through an opening between the stones as the figure started up the beach. She struggled and tried to cry out again, and Hobart Weatherby punched her in the stomach. She felt the searing pain take away her breath. Held by Bob Weatherby's tight grip, she could only gasp into his hand and let the pain in the pit of her stomach subside. The figure disappeared from view for a moment and then came back into sight between the rocks. As she saw the tall form, the unruly shock of hair falling over his forehead, she felt herself gasp incredulously. Ted! It was Ted, she repeated to herself. It was impossible and yet he was there, walking toward them, scanning the rocks.

He was getting close now. Opening her mouth, Jean came down hard on a finger. Bob Weatherby's roar of pain was gratifying, and she felt his hand come away from her mouth.

"Ted! Look out!" she screamed into the wind. She saw Ted whirl but Hobart Weatherby was racing out from behind the rocks at him, and she saw Ted duck away from a roundhouse blow. Bob Weatherby had left her and was racing out now, too, as Ted sent the older man down with a short uppercut. As Ted turned, Bob Weatherby tackled him and both men went down to roll and struggle on the ground as a sheet of water crashed down over them.

She saw Hobart Weatherby get up slowly and then she glimpsed the gun in his hand, dull-blue and menacing. He circled the two men wrestling on the ground and then, his arm upraised, he brought the gun down sharply and the struggling figures ceased their struggles. She saw Bob Weatherby slowly rise and Ted's limp form lay still, and she was running, brushing past Hobart Weatherby, kneeling down beside Ted, cradling his head in her arms.

She looked up to see Hobart Weatherby leveling the gun at her.

"No," Bob said, putting a hand on the older man's arm. "Stay with the way we planned it. There'll just be two of them found here, if they're found at all. No questions, no investigations."

The older man, his sharp, darting eyes losing their insane glitter, lowered the gun. "Yes, you're right." he said. "He'll never leave here any more than she will."

Jean watched the two men turn and run back to where their dory lay on what was left of the shoreline of the island. She watched as Hobart Weatherby paused, and she heard the four shots ring out as he put two holes in each of the other boats. Bob pushed their dory from the pebbled edge of the island and the sea swept it out at once, lifting it high and carrying it off. She got a last glimpse of them as they rode the tossing waves and then she was alone with Ted, looking down at the line of red on his temple where the gun butt had struck. The sea flung itself against the island as if to wipe it from its path, and the water was rising fast. She cradled Ted's head in her arms as the rain began to come down in furious, wind-driven sheets, mingling with the ocean's blows. In another hour, perhaps less, the sea would inundate Rock Island, sweeping over it with overwhelming fury that would leave nothing alive. The rain slammed into her on the edge of the wind, and she felt Ted move, lift his head and, his eyes snapping open, struggle up at once.

"They've gone," she said simply, meeting his eyes. "They shot holes in the boats. They're useless to us."

Ted rose, a little unsteadily and then straightened out as she helped steady him. He looked down at her and found a grin. "You know, you're a problem to people, girl," he said, and she felt something that was neither sea spray nor rain or her cheeks.

"Ted, Ted, what are you doing here?" she said, leaning her face against him.

"Seems I've heard that before," he said, and she nodded into his chest. She looked up at him.

"What does it all mean? Why Bob and his father? Am I dreaming all this?" she asked.

"I wish to hell you were," Ted answered. "I was halfway back to Boston when it hit me. I turned around and came back. I got there just as the Weatherbys were pulling out of the harbor. It wasn't hard to figure where they were going and why."

"It is for me," she said. "The why part of it."

"That night when he tried to kill you in the fog," Ted said. "I'd promised to call Bob Weatherby back when I heard something, remember?" Jean nodded. "The first thing he asked was whether you'd been hurt," Ted went on. "It bothered me then, but it didn't really register. I kept thinking about it as I drove back yesterday and all the things I'd learned about the Weatherbys kept pounding at me and then, suddenly, the phone call registered and it all hung together. I'd only told him you'd been picked up by the patrol boat. I hadn't told him about the rest of it yet when he asked about you being hurt. He had no reason to ask that then, not unless he knew there was every chance you might be, which of course he knew. All the rest made sense once and for all. The Weatherbys own Hawk's End. Every one of the fishermen is in their debt, either through bank loans, mortgages, or grocery credit. They raise prices whenever they feel like it and squeeze the people dry. The Weatherbys were the real losers by your opening the cove to fishing. They were the ones who stood to gain by the poor state of the fishing trade. Prosperity could wreck their little monopoly. They worked it so the people have just enough to struggle by with and pay their high interest rates, their overcharging for gasoline and groceries and not enough to get out from under their grip. It's not a new practice. It's been done many times before in many places. The Weatherbys just have their own version of it."

"I suppose when I suddenly popped up it threatened their whole little empire," Jean said. "That's why there was all that business about waiting to get a government report. It was a delaying action."

"That's right," Ted said. "They thought if you'd pack up and leave in a few weeks everything would go back to business as usual, with them controlling things for a practically nonexistent owner. But you went and got involved, and they saw you were going to upset the whole apple cart."

A lot of the little things fell into place now, Jean thought back grimly. Bob's suggestions that she leave, his concern for her safety, wanting her to tell him wherever she went, and even the long ride in the afternoon. It had enabled Hobart Weatherby to plant the false note from Amantha.

"But they've won anyway, Ted," she said, looking up at the long, lanky man beside her. "I'm just sorry you're here. It's not your fault, none of it."

"Maybe they haven't won yet," Ted said grimly, his eyes sweeping the moving mountains of foam-flecked green.

"The sea will sweep over this place completely," Jean said. "We've not much time left, a half-hour or so, perhaps."

She felt his arm around her waist and he was looking down at her, his smile tinged with sadness.

"How about you, Jeanie girl? Have you those answers you had to find?" he asked.

"Some of them," she said. "I think you were right about my guilt. I was trying to punish myself, at first, anyway. It's a funny thing, guilt. Nothing outside can get rid of it for you. No one else can meet it for you. You've got to meet it inside yourself, meet it and know it for what it is or it'll rule you. I know that now."

"And the other things?"

She met his eyes, her face grave, solemn. "They're still there, still unanswered. Maybe they never will be," she said. "But something more than the Weatherbys has been at work here."

Ted shook his head at her. "That's what I like about you, girl," he said. "You never let logic interfere with your stubbornness."

She leaned her head into his chest and then a tremendous wave crashed over the rocks, coming down on them to swirl around for a moment and then rush out to join the sea. More like that one would be coming now, she knew, and looking up, she saw the piece of wood float out from among the rocks behind them. About three feet long, splintered and charred at both ends, it came to a halt near where they stood, and Jean read the lettering on it, black with a faint gold edging. Her lips parted, she looked up at Ted and then picked up the wood. The lettering blazed out at her and she read it again, aloud. "Fiona MacFie," she gasped and saw Ted's eyes narrow, looking at the piece of planking.

"It's from the bridal boat, Ted," she said excitedly as she turned it over, examining it.

"It could be, it just could be," he said slowly. She ran her fingers along the charred ends of the wood. Had it been lodged here on Rock Island for over a hundred years, swept here after the fiery craft had burned itself into the sea? Or did this remnant of that terrible night still blaze with an undying spirit?

"Come on," she heard Ted's voice say crisply as another towering wave swept over them. She looked up to see him peering across the heaving water and there, moving toward them, heeled over in the near-gale winds, was a fishing trawler.

"Mount Rushmore," Ted said laconically, feeling the girl's wide-eyed, wondering stare. "He was on the wharf when I got back, and I gave him a fast rundown on what was going on. He told me how you'd run from him. But the Weatherbys had cleared the harbor by then, and he wanted to come with me in the dory. I vetoed that. There was no guarantee I'd make it, or we'd make it. We'd be running ten minutes or so behind the Weatherbys, and the sea was building so fast that ten minutes could spell the difference between making it and not making it. He agreed to round up a crew and take one of the trawlers. That way, if I didn't make it, maybe they could still get here in time. And if I did, I knew we'd need them to get us the hell off here which, girl, is what I'm about to do."

As if to add emphasis to his words, a series of waves swept over the rocks, deluging them with swirling, choking force. She felt Ted's hand holding her up as the sea pulled on her, and then they were free of the water for a few moments again. One of the boats had been swept out to sea. The other was still clinging to the land by its nose.

"Let's go," Ted said. She started running with him, clutching the piece of splintered planking to her.

"What do you think you're going to do with that?" Ted yelled at her.

"Take it with me," she said.

"Don't be ridiculous," he said. "You'll have enough to do to save your own neck."

"I'm taking it," she said, holding it to her breast, glaring up at him. "It's important to me."

"You're a dammed menace," he said. "Get in the boat."

"But it's no good," she protested. "I told you, Weatherby shot holes in it."

"It'll last a few minutes, long enough to get us further out. They can't come in any closer with that trawler," he said. He leaped into the boat beside her as another wave swept the island, lifting them from the shore and sending them swirling out to sea. She saw the waves driving onto the rocks now, piling over them in mounting succession. Ted yanked the motor on but the propeller was more often out of the water than in, and they were swept helplessly along by the mountainous waves. She saw the big trawler, too heavy to crest the seas as the dory did, shudder as a tremendous wave smashed into it.

"We're going to pass too far astern," she cried out and saw Ted's grim face echo her fear.

"They can't come about in a tight enough circle to intercept us, not in this sea," he commented. "They'd be set on their beam ends instantly."

The trawler took another crashing wave, and then Jean saw the boat start to move backward. "They've reversed engines," she said, and Ted nodded, his eyes gauging the distance.

"Get ready," he said as the trawler neared them, the stem moving across their path. But they were still too far away and taking in water fast. They disappeared in a trough, and when they came up Jean saw the figures at the stern rail of the fishing vessel.

"We'll never do it," Jean said. "This sea will slam us so hard against the trawler it'll break every bone in our bodies."

"If we stay in the dory it will," Ted said. "But we're not staying in it. It's about to sink under us anyway. Heads up, now." Jean followed his gaze and saw the lines hurtle from the trawler, first one, then another. Both fell short and were hauled in again. The next time they whistled through the air and Ted caught them, one at a time. He tied the first one around her waist, looping it under her armpits and securing it at her waist. She still clung to the piece of planking and he glared at her.

"Jump!" he said. "Tread water if you can. They'll pull you in." He gave her a helping shove, and then she was in the icy water, rising up on the crest of a towering wave, then coming down again. She looked around frantically and saw Ted's bobbing head behind her. She felt the line pulling her forward, and she blew air into her lungs at a brief moment before the sea covered her again. The side of the trawler was looming up in front of her now, and as a wave lifted her, rushing her toward the steel plates of the ship, she felt herself swung into the air at the last moment. Seconds later she was being pulled over the rail of the ship, gasping for breath, her arms still clutched around the piece of planking.

She was sitting up against the small cabin when Ted was swung aboard. Then he was beside her, and she looked up and found him grinning down at her.

"Haven't I met you someplace?" he said, and she let herself study the line of his long face, the cool, amused eyes that she had looked into so often and had seen so little.

"Yes," she said finally. "You're someone I thought I knew. But you're really someone I've got to start knowing all over again." He held her eyes with his, his lips just edged with a smile.

"Hope you'll enjoy it," he said.

"Yes, I think I will," she said slowly. "I think I will."

The trawler shuddered, heeled over and righted itself. She saw men bending to their tasks, holding on for life, wearing lifelines around their waists. Ferris was among them somewhere, she knew. He must have fought desperately to get a crew together to go to Rock Island, and she was terribly grateful to him, grateful and ashamed of herself. She stayed against the cabin, out of the way of the wind and the sea and the crew. Finally, after tossing and turning and just avoiding the fullest fury of the storm, the ship reached the small harbor. Rounding the breakwater, it slowed in the calmer waters. When they moored, a hard and difficult task in the strong, windswept waters of the harbor, Ted got to his feet and pulled her up.

"I'll meet you at the car," he said. "It's at the head of the wharf." He took the piece of planking, prying it gently from her grip. "I'll take this for you," he said. "I'll be very careful with it."

Then he was gone. The rain, driving hard now, blotted out his long form as he hurried down the wharf. She waited beside the rail of the ship as the crewmen left. Ferris was last, and he halted in front of her, his face unsmiling, his eyes boring into her.

"I'm sorry," she said to him. "I was too frightened to think anything through."

"You're safe now. That's what counts," he said.

"I'm going back to Boston, Ferris," she said as they faced each other, unmindful of the rain that whipped down on them.

"I never wanted anything else," he said, and she searched his unwavering eyes. "I don't want things that can't be."

"You always knew that, didn't you, that we could never be," she said softly.

"What we could give each other isn't enough for what we couldn't," he said simply. He turned and stepped to the wharf. He didn't look back.

Jean went up the wooden boards, to the waiting dark green car. She got in and put her face against Ted's shoulder, and she felt terribly tired and terribly sad and terribly happy all at once.

"Let's go back, Ted," she said.

"Best idea I've heard yet," he said. "I've already called the police. They're picking up the Weatherbys right now. You won't have to come back till it's time for the trial. The police will send a man down to get your sworn statements till then."

Ted swung the car up the hill that led from town and onto the dune road. The wind whistled, and the gray bulk of the house at Hawk's End stood stark against the storm. It seemed, as she watched, to be making a last defiant stand against the winds and the rain that tore at it. The malevolent, evil presence of it no longer pulled on her. It was simply a battered old derelict of a house. Ted turned the car away, and she closed her eyes as they drove home.

CHAPTER EIGHT

The doorbell rang, two short rings, and Jean ran to press the buzzer. That would be Ted. She had martinis ready, as she'd had every day for the past three weeks. As she went to open the door her eyes lingered on the charred piece of planking where it stood against the wall.

"Hi, honey," she said as Ted swept her up in an embrace that lifted her from the floor. His lips on hers were softly insistent with the promise she had come to wait for with a wonderful wanting.

He put his camera and an envelope of prints on the table as she poured the drinks. When she handed him his, he gave her a knowing little smile.

"What's happened, Jeanie girl?" he asked, and she looked at him blandly.

"Happened? Nothing's happened," she said.

"Don't play games with me, sweetie," he said. "I can see it in your eyes. There's a haunting in them again."

She grimaced. He knew her too well. "I got the letter from the laboratory," she said. He leaned forward and ran his hand along her face.

"You said you wouldn't be disappointed if you didn't hear what you thought you would," he reminded her. "What did they say?"

She glanced over at the planking against the wall, the name Fiona MacFie hand-lettered across the top of it. When they had returned she'd insisted on sending a piece of it to MIT for dating tests. He had called her absolutely stubborn and pigheaded, but, of course, she had gone right ahead and now, the letter was burned into her mind. She'd read it a dozen times since opening it that morning.

"They said the wood was too recent for use of the carbon fourteen dating process," she said. "But using a combination of other methods they agreed that the wood was approximately a hundred and fifty years old."

"That fits in," Ted said. "There's no question that it's a piece from Fiona MacFie's bridal boat then."

"No, there's no question of that," Jean said. "But the charred part tested as having been charred within the last four weeks or so. What's more, the charring had strange qualities to it they couldn't identify, 'an unusual molecular arrangement,' they said."

Ted's eyes were serious, unsmiling as he looked at her for a long moment. "The other world again," he said. "Forces that communicate and transmit, that call and command."

"They exist, Ted," Jean said. "They exist. They existed there at Hawk's End, along with the logical, the explainable."

"Being possessed, that exists, too?" he probed.

"Yes, until you free yourself somehow," she answered. "It exists, too."

He lapsed into silence again, and then he spoke slowly, carefully, weighing each word as though it were gold.

"Yes, I believe it does," he said, and Jean felt her eyebrows rocket upward.

"What's made you change your mind?" she asked.

"Because I've been possessed," he said. "By you, dammit. And what's worse, I don't want to get free of it at all."

His grin flashed out at her, and she landed in his arms. "You're incorrigible," she said. "And I'm glad you're possessed."

www.ingramcontent.com/pod-product-compliance
Lightning Source LLC
LaVergne TN
LVHW051005080826
845145LV00009B/2466

* 9 7 8 1 9 5 7 8 6 8 3 6 3 *